MYSTERY MEN
(& WOMEN)

AIRSHIP 27 PRODUCTIONS

Mystery Men (& Women) Volume five

"Not That Kind of a Girl" ©2017 Gene Moyers
"Lost in the Flood" ©2017 Thomas Deja
"The Death Ray" ©2017 Michael Black & Ray Lovato

An Airship 27 Production
www.airship27.com
www.airship27hangar.com

Cover illustration ©2017 Ted Hammond
Interior illustrations ©2017 Rob Davis

Editor: Ron Fortier
Associate Editor: Fred Adams Jr.
Marketing and promotion: Michael Vance
Production and design by Rob Davis.

ISBN-13: 978-1-946183-30-9
ISBN-10: 1-946183-30-X

Printed in the United States of America

10 9 8 7 6 5 4 3 2 1

MYSTERY MEN
(& WOMEN) VOLUME 5
—TABLE OF CONTENTS—

(A Shrike novella)
By Gene Moyers

*A mysterious figure in black appears on the scene to rescue a struggling reporter and then recruits her as one of her operatives. Who is the **Shrike** and what is the real meaning behind her crusade against crime?*

(A Nightbreaker Adventure)
By Thomas Deja

Nightbreaker battles a super powered killer who commands water, thus able to drown his victims at will.

(A Doc Atlas Adventure)
By Michael Black & Ray Lovato

1946 New York, an evil genius using Nikla Tesla's notes, has created a death ray and is threatening to destroy the Statue of Liberty unless paid a huge blackmail ransom. Can the Golden Avenger and his men solve the mystery of the Dark Destroyer before it is to late to save Lady Liberty?

NOT THAT KIND OF A GIRL
(A NOVELLA)

By Gene Moyers

Delores Dickson typed the last period of her article, sat back and stared wryly at her typewriter. She shook her head and cranked the typewritten sheet out of the machine: The report on the Morgan-Simpson wedding. Two years out of *Brooklyn College* and this is what her journalism degree had earned her, writing fluff pieces for the society section. The attractive blonde tucked the article into a file folder and stood up thinking sardonically to herself, "Another fine piece of journalistic work; my professors would be proud." As she sighed and glanced toward her editor's office, she saw his heavy set form crossing the busy city room in her direction.

Fred Sims was in his usual uniform; jacket off, white shirt with the cuffs rolled up and a pencil tucked behind his right ear into his thinning brown hair. He carried a piece of paper and pointed toward Delores as he pushed past the desks of reporters talking into phones or banging away on their typewriters. She sighed and sat back down in her chair wondering what kind of boring assignment he had for her now. As he reached her Sims pasted what he thought of as his friendly, fatherly expression on his face, "Dixie, just the gal I'm looking for!"

Although born in South Carolina Delores' family has moved north when she was seven. She soon lost most of her accent but her childhood nickname had stuck and no one ever called her anything but "Dixie."

She gave him a weary smile back, "What is it this time, Fred, a society wedding or a dog show?"

Sims looked hurt, "C'mon Dixie. You know I save the plum assignments for you. Besides it's not the wedding season." He brandished a sheet of paper. Dixie took it. It was a letter requesting an obituary to be placed in the paper. Dixie groaned inwardly as she skimmed the letter, grumbling, "Is George on vacation again? I hate doing obituaries!"

Suddenly Dixie sat up straight in her chair, Sims' excuses unheard. She interrupted him, "Is this right?"

He faltered, "Is what right?"

"The name? No, never mind! Okay, I'm on it!"

Sims mouth dropped open as Dixie stood up and brushed past him. He watched confused as she hurried away. Knowing how Dixie hated these kinds of assignments and was always bothering him for "serious" news work he had expected a lot more opposition. Sims scratched his head as he headed back to his office, "Women, who can understand 'em?"

Dixie made for the stairs and hurried down two floors. She passed the publication's morgue and quickly reached the small obituary room. The small windowless office contained nothing but file cabinets and a small table. Every major newspaper kept obituaries on file for important personages: politicians, the famous, business leaders and of course, the wealthy. Periodically these were updated so that if someone important died an obituary was already on file ready to use. Dixie had spent several days updating obits, as they were known, the summer before when the usual reporter who handled them was on vacation. She made straight for the "W" drawer. In less than a minute she had found the narrow file marked George Weatherby. Leaving the office she returned to her desk, reading as she went.

Dixie had recognized the name instantly when she had glanced at the letter. George Weatherby fell into more than one category of important people. He was the owner of one of New York's largest shipping firms. In addition to the shipping line he was major importer-exporter and owned interests in railroads, banks and even a commercial trucking company. While skimming the paper daily, she had read several articles regarding Weatherby and his business empire.

Grabbing that morning's *Bulletin* she quickly scanned through the news section. She found the article on page four; a one column item entitled "Local businessman killed in freak accident." Dixie leaned forward over the paper and quickly absorbed the article. Two days before Weatherby's auto had been struck by a loaded fork lift. He had been killed instantly. The accident had happened on the docks during work hours and there had been plenty of witnesses. Police were conducting a routine accident investigation. She sat back in her chair. *An accident?* Dixie felt the itch at the back of her neck that told her something was up; kind of a strange accident. She grabbed her phone.

Dialing a number she knew by heart she was soon connected to one of New York's numerous police precincts. Finally the phone rang through and was answered, "Twelfth precinct, Detective Keegan."

"Hello Pat. How's your day going?"

"Dixie! How's my favorite reporter?"

Dixie made a rude noise, "Pshaw, some reporter I am. The only things I get to report on are flower shows and celebrity birthday parties!"

"Oh, it's not that bad. I'm sure you'll get the chance to do more news stories soon. Remember that fire on 53rd last year?"

"The *Bulletin* had to accept my story. But if I hadn't been passing by and gotten them the scoop, I'd have been out of luck, as usual." There was a pause and when Dixie continued, there was sugar in her voice, "But you might be able to help with a big story, Pat."

On the other end of the phone Detective Pat Keegan scratched his head thoughtfully. When Dixie used that tone it usually meant trouble for someone, probably him if he got involved. On the other hand he might be able to turn this to his favor. "Uh, huh, just what do you need this time?"

"What do I need this time? You act as if I only call when I want something," Dixie demanded.

"Now, Dixie, you know I'd like to see more of you but it seems that most of the time when we see each other it involves you chasing a story."

Dixie pouted a little, "You're just trying to make me feel guilty. You know I like spending time with you, Pat. I just need one small favor." She paused and whispered conspiratorially, "I'll tell you what; if you help me out we'll go out as soon as I can get free."

Pat sat up straight, "Dinner."

"Uh, how about lunch? I can get free for that any time."

"Nope, it's dinner or nothing."

Dixie sighed, "Okay, dinner."

"Good, what do you need?"

"Okay, two days ago there was a traffic accident down on the docks. Apparently a fork lift hit a car and killed the owner. He was a George Weatherby, a big wheel in shipping. What I need to see is the police report."

There was silence for a moment before the detective answered, "That's another precinct."

"But you can get it, can't you?"

"It may take a little time. But yeah, I can get it."

"Good, call me when you do." Dixie thanked him and hung up. Thoughtfully she revised Weatherby's obituary and dropped it on her editor's desk. She then started asking around. It didn't take long to find a business reporter who knew a lot about Weatherby. She took copious notes before thanking him and heading for the paper's morgue to locate some articles about the deceased. By the time she broke for lunch Dixie had a pad full of notes and a good idea of the extent of Weatherby's financial empire. She grabbed her purse and went to lunch, her mind running through stories.

When she returned an hour later there was a message for her telling her to call Detective Keegan. She smiled and dialed his number. They made arrangements to meet and she got back to her research.

At five that evening she met Keegan outside of his precinct house. He had a slim file for her, "This is a copy and I need it back."

Dixie smiled up at the young detective as she tucked the file into her oversized purse, "Thanks Pat, I owe you."

"And I intend to collect...soon."

Dixie leaned in and kissed him on the cheek then turned toward the taxi waiting at the curb. Touching his cheek where she had kissed him Keegan yelled after her, "Don't lose that file!" She waved as the taxi accelerated away.

• • •

The next day Dixie was down on the docks nosing around. She had spent the night before going over the file and thinking. The description of the accident and the eyewitness statements seemed clear enough but still seemed odd to her. Now she had come to see for herself. She very much wanted to talk to Frank Valente, the driver of the forklift. There was no physical evidence left at the accident site but Dixie could still get a good look at it. It was a wide intersection between warehouses with good visibility. It was also busy. Trucks and forklifts passed by regularly and dock workers passed by continually. Certainly someone must have seen the accident. Unfortunately none of the dozen or so men she spoke to had actually seen the accident, although everyone had heard of it.

Frustrated, Dixie left and looked for the *North Atlantic & Gulf* shipping office where Valente was employed. Ironically this was Weatherby's own shipping line. At the office she was told that Valente had called in sick. Frowning, Dixie asked for his home address. There was some hesitation but money changed hands and she soon left the office with the address.

Taking a bus she reached the brownstone where Valente lived within a half hour. Her ring at his doorbell was not answered. She then rang the manager who soon answered. When quizzed about Valente's whereabouts she stated, "No he's not sick that I know of. He told me he was going away for a few days."

Dixie hid her surprise and asked, "When was this?"

"Day before yesterday."

"Did he say when he would return?"

"'Fraid not, hun, sorry." Dixie thanked the manager and turned away. She headed back to the office determined to go back to the docks the next day.

Bright and early Dixie was back on the docks asking about the missing forklift driver. She had little luck. Although everyone seemed to know him, no one would admit to being a close friend. And certainly no one seemed to know where he was. Frustrated, she returned to the *Bulletin's* office.

Valente's absence only made Dixie more interested in talking to him so she began tracking down possible relatives of the missing dock worker. Later that afternoon her phone rang. She held the earpiece to her ear and leaned toward the candlestick phone as she continued sorting through papers, "Dickson."

A rough voice replied, "Are you the skirt who's asking around about Frank Valente?"

Dixie sat up straight, "Yes I am. Do you know where he is?"

There was a slight pause, "I might. What's it worth to ya?"

Dixie gritted her teeth and quickly thought about the cash in her purse and her bank account, "I might be able to come up with a few dollars. Who are you?"

The voice replied, "It don't matter. But I can use some dough. If you want to know where Valente's hiding out, yah got to meet me tonight."

Dixie's eyebrow rose, "What's Valente hiding from?"

"I can't talk now. Meet me tonight at Hansen's Diner. Water Street; lower east side. Eleven o'clock. Got it?"

Dixie was scribbling furiously, "How will I know you?"

"Hang around out front. I'll see you from inside and come out to meet you"

"But what—" The line went dead. He had hung up. She sat back in her chair and thought. Obviously word of her looking for Valente had gotten around. So, who was this? One of his friends…or someone who didn't like him? It didn't really matter as long as he could help her find Valente. His mysterious disappearance made the accident all the more suspicious. Eleven was a little late for a meeting but a public diner seemed safe enough.

• • •

At eleven o'clock that night Dixie was walking up to Hansen's Diner. Hansen's was a busy place at that time of night. With workers loading and unloading ships around the clock less than two blocks away it wasn't unusual for them to be busy at odd hours. Through the window Dixie could see that most of the customers were roughly dressed dock workers and sailors. She was receiving a good bit of attention from them. Probably not many well-dressed, attractive women were seen in that neighborhood at night. Used to being looked at Dixie stayed calm and waited.

Soon a stocky man with his cap pulled low on his head pushed his way through the door. As he reached her he spoke, "You the dame?"

Dixie nodded, "I am. Let's go inside, I'll buy you a cup of coffee while we talk."

The big man looked around furtively, "No. I don't want to be seen spilling' to yah. Let's walk." He turned and walked down the sidewalk. Dixie frowned but hurried to fall in step with him. As she did she glanced at him, "What's your name? And why all the mystery?"

The big man looked at her and still walking reached and grasped her left arm at the elbow. Startled, Dixie tried to pull away. As she did, a strong hand grasped her right wrist in a powerful grip. Turning she saw another roughly dressed man. She drew breath to scream for help but before she could the second man clapped a hand across her mouth. Between the two of them they lifted the helpless female reporter nearly off her feet and dragged her rapidly down the block.

Dixie was furious. She struggled but her feet were barely touching the ground and her arms were locked up tight by the much larger men who had captured her. Nearly a block from the diner the two pulled up short next to a dark sedan. The man on her left used his free hand to jerk open the rear door. He pulled Dixie toward the darkened interior but was brought up short by resistance from the thug holding her other arm. For a brief second Dixie felt like a turkey wishbone as her arms were stretched painfully between the two roughnecks. The man holding her right arm swore and said, "What the heck is that?"

Both Dixie and her other captor looked toward the car's front end. It was dark on the sidewalk next to the car but Dixie could clearly make out a long thin rod of some sort sticking out of the flattened front right tire. The second thug let go of her arm and stepped forward. Before Dixie could break away she felt a sharp poke in her lower back and a harsh voice spoke in her ear, "Just stand still sister unless you want blood all over that pretty dress." Dixie gritted her teeth and waited.

Bending forward the second thug grasped the rod and spoke in a surprised tone, "Hey it's an ar—"

He was cut off as a dark clad figure glided swiftly out of the shadows next to the building and swung an arm at his head. He jerked his head at the last moment but was struck hard enough for Dixie to hear the thump. He went down in a heap against the car's fender. The figure spun toward

Dixie and her captor. In the dim light Dixie could see that the newcomer was dressed head to foot in what appeared to be dark, close-fitting clothes. He did not wear a hat but his features were concealed by a tight-fitting hood that completely covered his head. He appeared to be wearing a sash of some sort running from hip to shoulder and a staff of some kind stuck up behind his head. He carried something in his gloved right hand. Dixie was so startled by this sudden appearance that she didn't attempt to escape. It made no difference though as her captor gave her a powerful shove that sent her sprawling to the sidewalk.

As she steadied herself on her hands and knees Dixie watched as the roughneck crabbed forward, a long knife in his hand. He grated out from behind clenched teeth, "Who the heck are you?"

The masked man did not answer. Instead he seemed to sink a little bit in height and waited. The thug did not repeat his question but instead lunged forward, the knife held low, blade up. The mysterious figure moved. He slid forward incredibly quickly, straight at his opponent. Dixie wasn't totally sure what happened next but it appeared he used his left forearm to brush aside the thrusting knife then pivoted to the left, brought his right hand across and down in vicious blow to land on his opponent's right forearm. The knife clattered onto the sidewalk. The big man let out a half curse, half gasp and grabbed his wounded arm. He tried to step back but the dark clad figure did not let up. He stepped forward and brought his forearm up and across the thug's face, his elbow connecting solidly to the thug's jaw. The big man swayed and dropped to his knees, whereupon the masked man snapped his booted foot forward into the dazed man's chest. The bigger man slammed back against the car. His head connected solidly with the car door and he slumped to the sidewalk, unconscious.

While this was happening Dixie scrambled to her feet. Before she could speak the masked figure grasped her hand and pulled her down the sidewalk. As they passed the front of the car the first thug lunged to his feet swinging his right arm in a wild, roundhouse punch at the mysterious figure. The masked man let go of Dixie's arm and ducked, the punch brushing his shoulder. As the thug pivoted with the force of his punch the dark clad stranger threw a vicious left jab into the bigger man's kidney. He then swung what Dixie could now see was a leather sap at the man's head. The thug collapsed to the sidewalk with a groan.

The masked figure grabbed her arm again. Dixie tried to pull away but the masked man spoke in a harsh whisper, "We have to keep going, there may be more around." Dixie recognized the sense in this and let herself be pulled along. The pair moved quickly to the corner and around it into a side street where he guided her toward a battered, dark-colored coupe. Opening the door, he pushed her in then glided around to the driver side. He removed the staff from his back and shoved it behind the seat, then quickly slid behind the wheel. He pressed the starter and the coupe turned over with a quiet growl. Shoving the coupe into gear he accelerated quietly away. Regaining her composure Dixie spoke up, "Just who the heck are you? And where did you come from?"

The figure kept his eyes on the road as he expertly guided the car uptown away from the docks. When he spoke it was in a muffled whisper, "I was nearby when they grabbed you. I didn't think they were taking you home so I intervened."

"But who are you and why were you there?"

"Actually I've been following you. I wasn't really surprised at what happened. You've been asking questions in the wrong places and you have obviously made someone nervous."

Dixie was annoyed. She hated being rescued. It ran against her sense of personal independence. "What do you mean you've been following me? Just who do you think you—?" Her eyes narrowed. That was the question wasn't it? She looked closely at the masked figure next to her. He really wasn't a particularly large fellow. Instead he had a compact athletic build. He was an expert driver who handled the amazingly quiet and powerful coupe competently and from what Dixie had seen he moved like a cat. She turned in the seat and asked forcefully, "Just who are you?"

The figure answered quickly, "That's not important now. What is important is that I want to know why George Weatherby was killed as much as you do." He braked and steered the coupe to a stop on a quiet street blocks uptown from the dock area. Turning off the engine he turned to look at Dixie. In the light from a nearby street light she could see that the tight fitting hood was a dark gray in color matching his tunic and pants. Across the cheeks of the hood were thick black bands of black adding to the sinister appearance of the mysterious stranger. She could see now that the sash across his chest was actually some kind of leather bandolier covered in flapped pouches containing God knows what. She could not make out the stranger's eyes in the dim light but she could feel him sizing her up.

"You're a good reporter, Miss Dickson, but you're asking the wrong questions. Questioning the fork lift driver is a waste of time. He is probably out of state by now. Instead you need to be asking why Weatherby was killed."

Triumphantly Dixie exclaimed, "Then he *was* killed, I knew something fishy was going on." She then looked suspiciously at her savior, "So…why was he killed?"

"My guess is it has everything to do with his shipping company."

"*North Atlantic & Gulf?*"

The masked figure nodded, "Yes. For some time now there have been increasingly successful smuggling operations going on in east coast ports. I have been tracking them, attempting to ascertain who is behind them. Lately they have been expanding. I believe they are attempting to link together operations in several major ports. Somehow Weatherby's company was involved. Perhaps he was part of the group. Perhaps he was being coerced into joining. I'm not sure. Certainly he was killed by the smuggling group. When you started asking questions about Weatherby's death, whoever is running this operation felt that you were a threat as well. That is why I intervened. Undoubtedly they wanted to find out what you knew and then there would have been an unfortunate accident."

Dixie had been in danger before but she still felt a slight chill as she realized what the stranger meant. She thought for a moment before asking, "So what now?"

"My investigation continues. If you wish to continue as well, I can use your help." He hesitated a moment before adding, "If you could break a story about a major east coast smuggling ring it might even convince your editor that you have more to offer than wedding reviews."

Dixie snorted, "Yeah, that would make old Sims eat crow wouldn't it? Hey, wait a minute! How do you know so much?" The figure replied calmly, "I know a lot of things. The question stands. Do you wish to work with me Miss Dickson?"

Dixie studied the figure for a moment before answering, "Well, I do sort of owe you. Besides, if this story is as big as you say— But what's your interest and who are you?"

The masked man spoke, "As I said my identity is not important. And I told you; I intend to close this smuggling ring down…permanently."

While Dixie thought, the masked figure spoke again, "If you decide to work with me I must tell you that it may be dangerous. The smart thing might be to just walk away."

Dixie thought a moment longer before nodding, "I've never been known for doing the smart thing…I'm in. What do you want me to do?"

"Good. Tomorrow you need to start researching Weatherby and his company. Find out everything you can. Financial status, clients, everything. Now that he is dead, there might be a breakup of the company or some kind of financial takeover."

Dixie nodded, "Okay, I've done some of that already. But maybe we should have questioned those two birds you thumped, not that you left much to be questioned."

A shake of his head, "They were just hired muscle. The man I'm after has plenty of money to hire whoever he needs to." The masked man started the car and pulled quietly onto the street. As they headed further uptown, Dixie thoughtfully studied her companion. He was silent as he guided the auto through the nearly empty streets. Suddenly she spoke, "You never told me what your name was."

He answered with silence. Frustrated Dixie shook her head, "So, I just yell 'hey you' when I want your attention?"

There was a pause and then he spoke quietly, "Some people have called me the Shrike."

Dixie shook her head, "Kinda theatrical don't you think?"

There was a slight chuckle, "Perhaps I like the spotlight."

Dixie had her own thoughts about that. She was about to speak again when they pulled over to the curb. She was startled to realize they were right in front of her apartment building. Dixie turned to the stranger who was holding out a folded piece of paper. Dixie took it as she opened her door. She stepped out but looked back into the darkened interior, "I'd ask how you knew where I lived but I'm afraid you just might tell me."

Another chuckle, "Never ask any questions you don't want to hear the answers to. I can be reached at the number listed on the paper. Send any reports to the address, and be careful. I'll be in touch." Dixie closed the door. In the brighter illumination of the street she could see that the coupe was a rather battered Ford coupe several years old. The mysterious driver shoved it into gear and it motored silently away. Dixie watched it thoughtfully for several moments before entering her apartment building. The whole incident seemed bizarre and a bit unreal. But it had happened. As she walked up the stairs to her apartment Dixie considered two things: one; her story was now going to be a lot bigger than she had thought and two; her mysterious savior was not a man at all. He was in fact a woman.

• • •

A tall, strongly built man, tough looking and roughly dressed pushed through the crowd of similarly dressed men toward a street car stop where still more men waited. As he reached the queue he turned as a voice called, "Hey Sam! What's your hurry? Some of us are going to get a beer."

The mysterious driver shoved it into gear and it motored silently away.

Although the man known as Sam cut a hulking figure in his rough clothes he had an intelligent look in his eye as he surveyed the speaker. His name was Tom and he was part of the crew that had 'Sam' had been working with that day. 'Sam', whose real name was Ronald, shrugged and shouldered his way toward where two men were waiting. He tucked his work gloves in a rear pocket of his overalls and spoke to the men, "Beer? Sure why not?"

Tom—a thin, wiry man—pointed down a street leading away from the docks, "There's a place down this way." He and the third man led Ronald to a run-down tavern that was a favorite watering hole for dock workers. It was crowded and smoky. The three elbowed their way to the bar where other laborers reluctantly made room for the newcomers.

Once their beers came the thirsty men took long swigs. Tom wiping his mouth with the back of his hand addressed Ronald, "You're a good man with your hands, Sam. You've loaded cargo before."

Ronald shrugged, "I've done a lot of things. What with jobs so scarce the last few years I've done everything from pick apples to driving truck, although I'm a mechanic by trade.

The third man nodded, "Yeah, jobs have been tough to find. But things are getting better. All the shipyards 'been hiring; especially with them big new battleships being built. Know any welding?"

Ronald nodded, "Done some. Maybe I should apply. I could use the money. Say, is there much overtime to be had around the docks?"

Sam nodded as he sipped, "Some. It depends on the company. Some are busier than others. I hear that *Southern Star* gets a lot of work; they're running a second shift that seems pretty busy. They're a rough crew over there though," he eyed Ronald's large bulk and shrugged. "You could probably hold your own."

Ronald said nothing as he sipped his beer. This *Southern Star Shipping* sounded like it might bear closer scrutiny. He waved his hand at the bartender to get another round for his friends. A little more alcohol might loosen their tongues.

• • •

Three days later in at a home in a fashionable neighborhood in North Boston a woman dressed in the black dress and white apron of a housekeeper held out a leather briefcase to a well-dressed, middle aged man putting on a top coat. As she did she smiled, "Here is your briefcase, sir. I will pick up your dry cleaning after my house cleaning and dinner will be ready at six."

The man smiled kindly at the middle-aged woman before him. Her mousey brown hair was done up in a bun that did not quite hide the first few streaks of gray. Her eyes were attentive behind her gold rimmed glasses. "Thank you Martha. I'll try to be here by six but I may have to work late…a lot has been happening at the office lately."

"Very well, sir. I'll keep dinner warm in the oven for you." The man placed his homburg on his head and turned to the door. As he walked down the front steps his housekeeper called after him, "Have a good day, sir."

With the front door closed the woman turned and headed toward the kitchen. Once there she removed her spectacles, placed them in a pocket of her apron and set to work. Within a half hour the kitchen was spotless. The breakfast dishes had been washed and put away. The counters sparkled. She proceeded into the dining room to continue her work. While she dusted she searched the room thoroughly, looking for anything unusual. Moving to the parlor she continued the dusting, straightening and sweeping, again checking behind paintings and furniture for anything out of the ordinary. Everything appeared in order as she moved toward the back of the house.

Entering what appeared to be a fairly large wood-paneled room the disguised Shrike looked around. This was Farley's study. Dusting and straightening as she went, the Shrike started a thorough search of the room. She quickly located a wall safe concealed behind a painting. It was locked and she wasted no time on it. Of more interest was the fireplace in one wall. It was early fall and no fire should have been burned there in months. Yet there were ashes in the hearth. On one knee the Shrike bent forward to examine them. She quickly ascertained that someone had burned a number of papers. She lifted several partially burned remnants and examined them carefully. When she was finished she carefully swept up the ashes and disposed of them in the trash. After washing her hands she was soon back in the study examining Farley's desk.

The desk was locked but this didn't slow the Shrike. She pulled a small leather case from her apron, removed a metal pick and had the desk unlocked in less than two minutes. She quickly found a loaded revolver in the right hand upper drawer and set it aside. She sorted through business documents, correspondence, personal memos even a child's school report card. She hesitated over this for a moment before moving on. Most interesting were several bank statements and a bank book she took more time with. After several minutes of studying the bank records she was more interested in what she did not find rather than what she did. When finished she replaced everything, re-locked the desk and finished her cleaning.

When finished downstairs the Shrike moved to the second floor. She didn't take long in the master bedroom making the bed and dusting efficiently. She carefully flipped through the hanging women's clothes noting empty hangars. She also looked over the hall closet carefully. She noted two empty spots among luggage stacked on the closet floor.

From there the Shrike moved to a smaller bedroom obviously occupied by a young child. When she had been interviewed by Mr. Farley to replace his housekeeper who had been called out of town, he had told the disguised Shrike that his wife and daughter were upstate visiting relatives for an extended time. The child's room was certainly unoccupied. The bed had been made and the room was neat and tidy. The Shrike immediately searched through the child's dresser and then her closet. She noted that her clothes were neat and ordered. Little seemed missing. On a small child's desk she noted school papers and books that she quickly sorted through. Standing back the Shrike shook her head.

Finishing her cleaning, the Shrike removed her apron, put on her coat and picked up her oversized matronly purse. As she reached the front door the letter slot near the bottom of the door clattered and several letters fell onto the hall rug. She picked them up and sorted quickly through them. All seemed to be bills or business correspondence except one. Moving into the kitchen the Shrike turned on the burner under the tea pot and waited. Within minutes the water was boiling away. Holding the letter carefully she waved it over the steaming vapor being careful not to get it too damp. Soon she placed the letter on a nearby counter and using a butter knife blade she carefully pulled open the letter's flap. Using two fingers she carefully removed the handwritten sheet within, unfolded it and quickly scanned the writing.

It was a personal letter in a woman's delicate script with the salutation "Dearest Oliver." and signed "Love Alice." It was from Farley's wife. She spoke of missing her home and family and then recounted her activities stating that her mother was much better and she would be ready to return soon. Interestingly she inquired about their daughter, Amy, and talked of how much she missed the little girl. The Shrike nodded her head. If the little girl wasn't with her mother, where was she? This would bear further investigation. Replacing the letter in its envelope she resealed it and placed all of the mail on Farley's desk. She then locked the house and walked to the corner.

She crossed the street, turned left and walked another block to the nearby elementary school. Entering, she made her way along the main hallway to the school office. She was greeted by the school secretary. She smiled at the woman, "I'm Mr. Farley's new housekeeper. He asked me to come by and pick up any new assignments so that he may forward them to his daughter."

The secretary seemed surprised and replied, "Really? Then she and her mother won't be returning soon?"

The Shrike smiled, "I'm not sure how long they've been gone or when they'll return. As I said, I just started this position."

"Yes, Mr. Farley was rather vague when he withdrew his daughter. Please wait while I speak with her teacher." She quickly bustled off. The Shrike waited patiently. She soon returned with a sheet of paper, "Here are all her assignments since she left." Taking it the Shrike thanked her and left.

At the corner she caught a bus and rode uptown. She picked up Farley's dry cleaning then entered a nearby drug store and went to the vacant phone booth in the rear of the store. Once inside she had the operator connect her with a long distance number. Soon the call was answered by a female voice, "Yes?"

"This is Shrike. Anything to report?"

"Yes. Ronald has successfully gained employment on the Philadelphia docks. He reports that he is making friends among the dock workers. He states that he is already tracking suspicious activities and will report regularly."

"Good. Anything from Dickson?"

"Yes. She has sent me detailed financial information on Weatherby's company. Apparently Weatherby's son is the sole heir to the company. She is arranging an interview with him. She also claims she has interesting evidence she will be forwarding soon."

"Good. When she contacts you give her the following orders." She continued with specific instructions and then hung up after promising the unknown voice further contact soon. She left the drug store and by two o'clock was back in the Farley residence.

· · ·

In New York Dixie left the newspaper building and waved for a taxi as she reached the curb. Almost immediately one swerved out of traffic, ignoring angry horns from other drivers and screeched to a stop in front of her. Before the driver could hop out to open the rear door, the attractive reporter was already climbing into the rear seat. He turned around in his seat to stare at her legs and asked, "Where to, Miss?"

Dixie pretended not to notice his admiring glances and calmly gave him an address in mid-town. He nodded, dropped the flag and accelerated into traffic while leaning on his horn. The cabbie weaved in and out of traffic like a barnstormer as Dixie went over her notes. For two days she had been putting every spare moment into her assignment from the mysterious masked woman. Adding to what she already had learned, she spent hours speaking to business analysts and brokers about George Weatherby and his companies; especially *North Atlantic & Gulf Shipping*. She had also checked with state and local authorities about his business registrations, permits and licenses.

Once she had a good outline of Weatherby's business dealings—at least his aboveboard ones—she had called the phone number given to her and made arrangements to forward her report to the person who had called herself the "Shrike." A brisk female voice had answered her call. The voice had given her instructions to take a certain bus at a certain time. While riding the bus a woman had gotten on and taken the seat next to Dixie. The reporter had been surprised to find that this was not the same woman who had saved her from the two roughnecks. This woman was shorter, blonde and spoke with a more clipped accent than the dark-garbed woman. Dixie tried to get a good look at the woman as she passed the envelope of information to her but a large hat and veil frustrated her efforts. Accepting the envelope the veiled woman had instructed Dixie to continue her efforts and stand by for further orders. She had then gotten off at the next stop and disappeared in the crowd as Dixie watched from the bus window.

Dixie then dove into Weatherby's personal life. She discovered that he was widowed with only one son. He had been a driven man when it came to his business interests. He worked night and day with no hobbies or other outlets. It had shown in his business dealings. He ran one of the largest shipping empires on the east coast. Dixie had to wonder if the son would be able to fill his father's shoes. She made an attempt to get an interview with the younger Weatherby but he was not available.

While researching Weatherby, Dixie had found an unsettling pattern that had plagued *North American & Gulf* the last few months. There had been a series of accidents and unusual happenings that had cut into the efficiency of the shipping line. Men had fallen or been hurt in various industrial accidents. Two men had died. Ship sailings had been delayed. There had even been a fire in one *NAG*'s dockside warehouses. Dixie did some checking and found that Weatherby's insurance rates had gone up quite a bit in the last year. Sabotage? Blackmail?

These were the questions she would put to the man she was going to see now. She pushed through the revolving door of a high rise in mid-town and paused at the directory. Locating the correct firm she entered the elevator and asked the operator for the eighth floor.

Dixie exited the elevator and entered an office where she was politely received by a receptionist. Soon she was shown into the office of J. Thomas Mason. Mason was a lean forty-five year old man who had the look of a hard-driving executive. He also had been a senior manager and advisor to George Weatherby up until several months before when he had suddenly left the company. He rose and showed Dixie to a comfortable seat in front of his desk. Once settled he looked questioningly at the reporter, "Well, Miss Dickson, was it? What can I do for you?"

Dixie gave him her most charming smile, "Well, Mr. Mason, I'm researching an article on the late George Weatherby and *Northern Atlantic & Gulf*. Until recently you were employed there as a senior manager. I'm hoping you can give me some insights." She quickly noted the relaxed executive stiffen slightly at the name of Weatherby. He kept a neutral expression on his face though as he replied, "George's death was a terrible tragedy. Although if you're working that angle I'm afraid I can tell you nothing about his death except what I read in the newspapers."

Pulling out a notebook and pencil Dixie spoke, "Actually I'd like to ask about *North Atlantic & Gulf*."

"Oh, what would you like to know?"

Dixie looked him directly in the eye, "For starters I'd like to know why you left the company so suddenly. You were employed there for a long time and were a personal friend of George Weatherby if rumors are true?"

Dixie could see the gears turning in Mason's mind behind his carefully neutral expression. He paused before replying, "Yes, George and I were close. As for leaving, you said it yourself; I had been there quite a while. Perhaps too long, so when the opportunity for advancement came I took it. George and I parted on good terms."

Dixie scribbled busily and commented, "It looks like you have done well here. Do you have any comments on the accidents that seemed to have plagued *NAG* over the last year?"

Mason stiffened, "If you are implying that my management was flawed during my time at *North American* I categorically deny any responsibility for any of those tragic accidents!"

Dixie's eyebrows rose, "No one is implying anything, Mr. Mason. I'm just asking questions. It is interesting that you left the company just when it needed you." Mason's face turned red but before he could erupt Dixie changed the subject, "You were close to George Weatherby. Have you met his son?"

Caught off guard Mason closed his mouth and looked confused for a moment, "Uh, yes I've met young Matthew."

"What do you think of him?"

"Well, he's a bright young man, perhaps a bit headstrong."

Dixie added to her notes, "I understand he's employed at *North American & Gulf*. Is he prepared to step into his father's shoes?"

Mason looked rather suspiciously at Dixie, "Matthew is a contract negotiator. He traveled up and down the east coast arranging new contracts for his father, as well as surveying the competition at various ports."

"So he was just a salesman?" Dixie questioned.

Mason blustered, "No, he was much more than that. And he could have been even more. His father was slowly grooming him for other things but Matthew preferred traveling."

Do you think he'll be prepared to handle *North Atlantic & Gulf* if this wave of bad luck continues to plague it?"

Mason frowned and then his face went very calm, "I believe young Weatherby will do just fine."

Dixie decided on a quick strike for reaction, "Did George Weatherby actually fire you?" Mason stood up angrily, "I think that will be all Miss Dickson. I have a very busy schedule today."

Dixie stood up to go and tucked her notebook into her large purse. As she reached the door she looked back with one hand on the knob, "Why did you really leave *North American & Gulf*?"

Mason looked hard at her, "George Weatherby and I were friends for many years. He cared for me and all of his employees. Anything he did, he did with good reason, as did I."

Dixie stared hard at the man for a moment then nodded and left the office. On her way down in the elevator she thought about her conversation with Mason. The man was a competent manager and had been close to Weatherby. He had certainly been aware of the hard luck the company was going through. Had he really left for better prospects or to protect his reputation? Or was it something else? One thing was certain, the man was hiding something. As Dixie crossed the building's lobby she decided it would be interesting to see Matthew Weatherby's reactions to his father's death.

Back in her office she made another phone a call to *North Atlantic & Gulf* for an appointment with Matthew Weatherby. It took a while to get his new secretary. When she did she was again told that the new head of North American was very busy and wasn't available for interviews. Dixie didn't push the issue. There were other ways get interviews. She hung up and grabbed for a telephone book, looking for Weatherby's home address. As she did her phone rang. She held the receiver to one ear and leaned forward toward the candlestick microphone while she continued to flip through the directory, "Dickson."

Clipped words came to her ear, "Miss Dickson? You have new instructions." Dixie grabbed for the phone as the directory slid to the floor, "Wait, I'm here!"

"You are to summarize any additional information on Weatherby and his enterprises at once. Place the information in a large envelope and leave it at the news stand in front of the *Empire Hotel* on 52nd Street. Second, you are to take a train to Boston as soon as possible. When you arrive take a room that has been reserved for you at the *Metrolite Hotel*. Await there for further instructions. Is that clear?"

Dixie struggled to hold the receiver while she scribbled down the information, "Yes, but what am I . . ."

"Your presence is needed. Can you leave by tonight?"

"Uh, yes, I think so."

"Good. You will be contacted." There was a click as the woman hung up. Dixie frowned. The voice had sounded more like the woman on the bus than the dark clad fighter she had met. Shaking her head and muttering, "What have I gotten into?" she wound a sheet of paper into her typewriter. Working from notes she began to type furiously.

Hours later Dixie waved down a taxicab outside of her apartment building. Inside she ordered him to take her to Grand Central terminal via 52nd. The cabbie turned to look at her in surprise, "That's kind of outa' the way, lady."

Dixie nodded calmly, "I have an important stop to make before I catch my train."

The driver shrugged, dropped his flag, and accelerated away. Traffic was fairly light and they made good time across town. As they approached the *Empire Hotel* Dixie reached forward and tapped the cabbie on the shoulder, "Pull over here."

The cabbie said nothing but pulled up smoothly in front of the entrance to the hotel. Before the doorman could reach the cab door Dixie was out and moving to the newspaper stand on the sidewalk. She carried a large stuffed envelope. Reaching the stand she glanced over the magazines briefly before choosing one and placed it and the envelope on the narrow wooden counter. The gray haired newsie running the stand smiled at her showing a missing tooth and said, "That'll be a dime, miss."

Dixie handed the man a dime and nodded. She took her magazine and turned back toward the cab. As she did she see the old man make the envelope disappear under the counter? Re-entering the cab, the cabbie leaned over the front seat and asked somewhat sarcastically, "That was your important business?" Dixie just smiled and held up the pulp magazine she had purchased, "I have a long trip ahead of me."

The cabbie shook his head, "Sure."

She settled back in the seat, opened her magazine and murmured, "My train leaves at eleven, you know . . ."

The cabbie was still shaking his head as he pulled away.

• • •

Oliver Farley closed the front door behind him. He hung his hat on the rack and put his overcoat in the hall closet. As he turned to the mail sitting on a side table in the hall his replacement housekeeper entered from the kitchen wiping her hands on her apron, "Good evening Mr. Farley."

The ship owner gave her a tired smile, "Good evening Martha."

"Your dinner is in the oven. You have your mail and I have left your phone messages on your desk in the study."

"That's fine Martha. You can go home now. Thank you for staying late today."

"It's just fine sir. I'll see you at the normal time tomorrow morning," The Shrike smiled as she opened the hall closet. She put on her coat and draped her large purse over her arm as Farley entered the kitchen. Opening the front door she left the house, firmly closing the door behind her. On the sidewalk she turned left and walked to the corner. Turning, she walked to the alley entrance, glanced around and silently entered the alley. Pausing a minute to allow her eyes to adjust to the darkness the Shrike slipped down the alley until she reached the back gate leading to the small back yard of the Farley residence.

Settling down into the deep shadow of a hydrangea bush she waited. A half hour later the lights in the kitchen and dining room went out. She waited ten more minutes before standing and moving quietly to the back door. She had made copies of the house keys and used one to let herself into the rear of the house. Standing in the entry she listened. At first there was near silence then came the sound of foot-steps and glass clinking.

She glided silently through the kitchen and turned into the main hallway. The only light on in the house came from the half open door to Farley's study. Silently she crept forward until she was just outside the study. Leaning forward slightly she could just make out Farley sitting behind his desk. He stared sightlessly downward. A decanter of whiskey sat on the desk and he had a glass of the amber colored liquid in his hand. As she watched he drained the glass and refilled it from the decanter. Before ducking back into the shadows the Shrike noted that his mail was untouched.

She had been in the household for nearly a week and she had seen enough to convince her that Farley was thoroughly frightened. His wife was out of town and he was encouraging her to stay away. His daughter was not at home and not with his wife. Where was she? The night before the Shrike had caught a one-sided conversation Farley had with an unknown person. The ship owner had been angry and frightened. He had tried to be defiant but had quickly been humbled by the unknown caller. There had also been the promise of a further call tonight. She settled in to wait.

Nearly a half hour passed. Farley had lowered the level of the decanter considerably when the phone rang. The Shrike drifted closer to the doorway as Farley answered the phone. She listened closely to the one-sided conversation:

"Yes, I'm alone. Is she there?"

A pause; "But you said I could speak to her tonight!"

Another pause; "I've already agreed to do everything you've asked! I've told you I'll do anything, just don't hurt my daughter!"

There was a longer pause then: "Amy! Amy, are you all right! No, don't cry baby! Everything's going to be fine, I promise!" In the shadowy hallway the Shrike nodded, her lips pressed tightly together and her face hard. It was as she had suspected. Farley's missing daughter was being held by someone as a tool to make Farley do as he was told.

Research around the Boston docks had led her to Farley's shipping company. Further research had convinced her that Farley was honest and unlikely to be involved in smuggling. Her suspicions were now confirmed.

Through an agent and application of cash the Shrike had convinced Farley's regular housekeeper to leave town on a temporary "family emergency." It had then been easy for the disguised Shrike to take her place temporarily. Now she had the final piece to Farley's involvement.

He stared sightlessly downward.

She listened as Farley tearfully made more promises of cooperation to the unknown kidnapper before hanging up. A last glance through the doorway before she glided silently away showed Farley face down on the desk his head cradled in his arms crying softly. The Shrike vowed that this wasn't how things were going to end.

•••

Dixie had arrived in Boston very late the same night she left New York. She took a taxi from the train station to the *Metrolite Hotel*. It was a modest hotel that catered to business travelers and salesmen. The sleepy night clerk readily admitted Dixie had a reservation and had the even sleepier elevator operator take her to the fifth floor and show her to her room. It was not much before dawn when she undressed and closed her eyes to sleep.

Rising rested the next morning, Dixie was ready to hit the streets. Unfortunately she had nothing definite to do. She was also mindful that she was to "wait for instructions." So she went out for breakfast and returned to her room to wait. She waited all day. She had never been to Boston and longed to explore the city but knew that as soon as she left the mysterious person known as "the Shrike" would call, so she waited. She went out once for lunch and a newspaper but otherwise never left the phone.

It was after nine that night when the phone finally rang. She grabbed it and spoke quickly, "Hello?"

"Miss Dickson?"

"Yes."

"There is a businessman in this city named Farley. His daughter has been kidnapped and is being used against him. Very probably by the man who is behind the smuggling ring. You must find out who took his daughter and where she is being held."

"Yes, of course. But where do I start?"

"You start at the Oakhurst elementary school. I have discovered that she was removed from the school by a ruse. Report to me at the usual number. Here is another number to use in case of emergency but it may not be answered at all times." Dixie quickly wrote down a local Boston number then asked, "What is the little girl's name and what does she look like?"

"Her name is Amy. She is eight years old. She has light brown hair and hazel eyes. I'm sure she must be very frightened. The sooner we can find her the better."

"Of course. I'll find her."

"I know you will. Now listen carefully. You are to locate the little girl but you are to take no action. No doubt the people holding her are very dangerous. When you have located where she is being held, call in and report. Then maintain a watch until I can reach you to effect a rescue. Do you understand?"

"Yes, I understand."

"Good. Report regularly." The line went dead as the Shrike hung up. Dixie hung the receiver back on the hook of the phone and started at it angrily. A little girl kidnapped. This was getting worse by the day.

• • •

The Shrike left the Farley house the way she had entered. Leaving the alley she made for a nearby bus stop. She traveled across town changing lines twice to be sure she wasn't followed before reaching the inexpensive rooming house where she was staying. She picked up her mail and went straight to her room. In that day's mail was the report that Dixie had mailed before she left for Boston. The Shrike had already digested Dixie's earlier report on the Weatherby's finances. This one contained information including the reports of accidents and possible sabotage. Even more interesting was her report on Mason, the former *North Atlantic & Gulf* executive.

When she finished reading Dixie's reports the Shrike made a phone call. She had paid extra to have a phone in this room. After her conversation with Dixie she placed another call. A female voice answered, "Yes."

"This is Shrike. Report."

Without hesitation the voice replied, "No word from Dickson since she left for Boston."

The Shrike replied, "I have spoken to Dickson and given her new orders. Stand by for telephone reports from her that may need to be forwarded immediately."

"Understood. Ronald has reported from Philadelphia. He is investigating the shipping firm he was led to. He states that it is employing shady people and is definitely up to no good. He is continuing surveillance and trying to get closer to the crew that works there."

"Good. Tell him that as soon as he has something concrete or if his situation becomes dangerous to pass on word immediately."

"Understood, standing by." The two women hung up almost simultaneously. The Shrike turned and walked to the window. She stared out the third floor window over into the empty street. The smuggler was working the

Boston docks through Farley's company. If she could find and return the little girl to her father, it would cripple his operations here. In Philadelphia, Ronald was onto something. Her instincts told her that the Philadelphia operation was probably more important. Rather than working through a proxy like Farley the smuggler might be present on the Philadelphia docks himself. She wanted to be there now but needed to wait until Dickson had located the little girl's location. Dickson was a competent investigator. Hopefully it wouldn't take long to track the kidnappers. Meanwhile the Shrike would continue to watch over Farley. When the time came she could reach Philadelphia quickly.

• • •

In Philadelphia Ronald had been busy. Working every extra shift he could wrangle he let it be known that he needed money badly. He had quickly made friends on the crews he worked with due to his hard work and open manner. After every shift he socialized with other dock workers at various water front gathering places. It took nearly a week but eventually he was approached by one of the men he wanted to get acquainted with. He was drinking a beer in a local watering hole near the docks when a well-built, blond-haired man squeezed in next to Ronald at the bar, "I hear you're looking to make some money?"

Ronald looked sideways at the man. He would have been fairly good looking if it weren't for his uncut hair, two days growth of beard and the hard, knowing look in his eye. Ronald took a sip of his beer before replying, "Maybe, if it ain't too crooked."

The big man sneered, "Oh, choosy, huh."

"Maybe. Depends on what I'm doing and how much it pays"

The blond man looked hard at Ronald evaluating him, "The pay is good and you'll just be workin' cargo like you're doin' now."

Ronald sipped and looked thoughtful, "Okay. So why's the pay so good then?"

"Because you do what you're told and keep your mouth shut."

Ronald nodded, "Okay. I got sick family. I can take a chance."

"Good, you workin' days now?"

"Yeah."

"Okay, tomorrow night. Eleven o'clock; meet me at warehouse eleven. I'll take you to meet the Boss." Ronald nodded his assent and waved for the bartender to bring a beer for his new friend.

The next night at eleven Ronald found his new friend, whose name was Donaghue, outside a darkened warehouse on the docks. They exchanged greetings and Ronald followed the big dockworker down a narrow, dimly lit street between two enormous warehouses. The two turned left and walked along the wide concrete loading pier that stretched north and south along the Delaware River. They passed a well-lit area where numerous dockworkers were loading a cargo ship to depart on the morning tide. They then passed another warehouse. Finally, they stopped. Ronald was about to ask where they were going when a man smoking a cigarette stepped out of the shadow of a towering stack of wooden pallets. He threw down his cigarette and stepped forward. Donaghue raised a hand in greeting, "Hey Boss. I brung the new guy I was tellin' you about." He jerked a thumb at Ronald. Ronald nodded to the new man as he studied him. He was tall, thin and dark-haired. In the dim light Ronald could not see much of his features but he could feel the man's hard stare. The man spoke, "What do they call you?"

Ronald gave him the name he had been using on the docks, "Sam."

"I've heard that you're a hard worker who can keep his mouth shut. Is that right?"

Ronald nodded, "Yeah, that's right."

"Are you any good with a hammer and saw?"

Ronald nodded again. With a further appraising look the thin man nodded and said, "Okay, we'll take a chance. Follow me." He turned and led the way between two warehouses toward the landward side of the building. Ronald followed, very aware that Donaghue was just behind him as they traversed the shadowy alley between the large warehouses. Once on the wide street and facing the landward side or "front" of the warehouse the thin man led them past the large, closed roll up doors to man sized door in the corner of the warehouse.

Pulling a ring of keys from his pocket he unlocked the door and they entered. Immediately Ronald could hear the sounds of men working. It was not deafening but he could identify hammers, saws and the thumps of heavy items being moved around. He could also hear multiple voices. All this came from beyond tall stacks of crates that blocked a direct view of most of the warehouse floor.

The thin man led them past the row of crates to the open floor of the warehouse. Ronald tried not to stare. A dozen men were hard at work. Nearby, four men were busy assembling large wooden crates. A man was cutting wood into set lengths while two men were busy hammering them together. A little further across the floor two men were busy stenciling black words onto newly-built crates and then stapling documents to the sides.

The thin man pointed at the crates being assembled and said, "You take over here. Joe and Frank will tell you what to do." He then yelled a name. One of the men came forward. The thin man told him to come with him and moved on with Donaghue following. Ronald shrugged and moved toward a half built crate. One of the men introduced himself as Frank, handed Ronald a hammer and gave him some quick instructions.

Ronald quickly went to work. He was assembling a crate that was about four and a half feet high, two and a half feet wide and eighteen inches deep. It was fairly easy work as long you knew one end of a hammer from another and Ronald quickly found a rhythm. As he worked he scanned the warehouse while trying not to be too obvious about it. He was counting bodies and memorizing faces. Further past the two men who were stenciling the assembled crates a man was wheeling a newly stenciled crate around a row of barrels on a hand truck. Ronald could hear voices from that area. A minute later the man returned with the empty hand truck. Obviously they were loading the newly built crates in that area near the river side of the warehouse.

When Ronald had finished hammering a crate together he used a hand truck to lift it and wheel it thirty feet to where the two men were stenciling them. They ignored him as he dropped it off and returned to his work. As he did Ronald got a good look at the words freshly stenciled on two sides of one of the new crates. There was a logo of some kind above three large letters: CRC. Below the letters were the words *Columbia Radio Corporation* in small letters. Thoughtfully, Ronald picked up his hammer and returned to work.

Columbia was a well-known radio manufacturer. His parents had one of their console models sitting in their living room even now. He nodded, thinking to himself that one of their console models would just about fit into one of the crates he was assembling.

So whatever was being smuggled was being sent out as radios. Ronald concentrated on doing a good job. He needed to become part of this group. There was information here that would be very interesting to the Shrike.

• • •

Standing outside the open garage door Dixie adjusted the angle of her hat before entering the gloom of the *Black and White Cab Company's* garage. She made her way past cabs and loud-voiced drivers to the dispatch office. Inside the tiny office a fat man, his coat off and sleeves rolled up, sat behind a battered desk. He was smoking a cigar and reading a newspaper. Waving aside the noxious smoke that filled the office Dixie asked, "Are you the dispatcher?"

The newspaper didn't shift but a voice came from behind it, "Who wants to know?"

Dixie summoned up her official voice and said, "My name is Dickson and I represent *New England Mutual Insurance*. I'm trying to locate an heiress that may have taken one of your cabs."

This time the paper came down and a man's suspicious face appeared over it, "Insurance?" He looked Dixie suspiciously up and down, "So insurance companies got dames doing their legwork now?"

Dixie ignored the remark and tried to look pleasant, "That's right and I'd like to know if you dispatched a cab to the Oakhurst elementary school on the 17th of last month."

The man lowered his paper to the desk and thought for a moment as he puffed on his cigar. Removing the cigar with one hand he spat in a spittoon and shrugged, "I don't know if we still got those logs."

Dixie did her best to continue smiling as she reached into her purse. She pulled two folded one dollar bills out and held them in front of her, "I'd really appreciate it if you could look for me."

The dispatcher put his cigar back in his mouth and reached out with a rough hand. Dixie handed him the money and watched as he made it disappear into a pocket. The dispatcher then walked to a file cabinet in the corner and began rooting around in one of the drawers. A minute later he pulled a sheet of paper out and read it over. Turning he held the paper out to her, "Sorry. We didn't dispatch a cab to any schools at all that day."

Dixie smiled weakly, thanked the man and left the office. Once on the street she pulled a notebook from her purse and crossed through a name on a hand written list. She had gone to the Oakhurst School that morning. Not wanting to raise any suspicions at the school she had instead canvassed the neighborhood. Several nearby neighbors remembered seeing a cab at the school that day and one remembered a little girl and a woman leaving in it. Dixie had sent up a mental thank you for busy body neighbors with too much time on their hands.

Unfortunately, further questioning had given her three different de-

scriptions of the taxicab that had taken the little girl away. So the ace reporter had gone to her best friend in such situations: the telephone directory. She had listed all the cab companies operating in Boston and was
working her way down the list. This was the second name crossed off. Next
up; *Checker Cab.*

It took her twenty minutes by street car to reach *Checker Cab* and her
luck was no better there, although she didn't have to bribe the dispatcher
as she had at the first two. She crossed *Checker* off her list and was walking
toward a nearby street car stop when inspiration turned a corner and drove
toward her. Dixie quickly stepped off the curb and waved down the approaching taxi. The taxi swerved toward her and pulled up. Dixie opened
the door with *City Cab Co.* printed on it and hopped in. The driver looked
over his shoulder and queried, "Where to Miss?"

Dixie gave him her best smile and said, "Actually I have business with
your dispatcher. Could you take me to your garage?" The driver looked
surprised then shrugged and said, "Sure thing, Miss." He turned around,
dropped the flag and leaned on the horn as he swerved back into traffic. He
weaved expertly in and out, ignoring the outraged fists that shook in his direction. Casually whistling as he drove the driver glanced over his shoulder,
"So you got business with Tony, eh? I hope it's not a complaint. Most of our
boys are pretty good drivers." He hesitated a moment before adding, "And
some of 'em are even polite."

Deciding that there might be an opening here Dixie leaned forward
and smiled, "Nothing like that. I'm just trying to locate a possible fare your
company might have picked up. "It's about a friend."

"Yeah? You looking for someone?"

"Yes…in a way. I believe my friend might be in trouble. If she is, I'd really like to help her." The driver thought about this for a moment before
answering, "Well, maybe I can help you. We'll be there in a minute." Dixie
leaned back patiently. Five more minutes and they were pulling up in front
of *City Cab's* garage.

The driver leaned over the front seat and said, "Tell ya' what, I'll go in
and talk to Tony. What's the address you're askin' about?" Dixie quickly
gave him the name of the school and the date. He hopped out of the cab
leaving it double parked on the street and went inside. Five minutes later
he was back. Once back in the cab he leaned over the front seat and said,
"Yeah, we took a call at that school on the 17th. My pal George took it."

A little surprised Dixie leaned forward, "Uh, that's great! Where do we
find your friend?"

"George usually works the downtown cab stands this time of day."

"Good. Can you take me there now?"

"Sure can. Hang on." He put the cab in gear and accelerated away. Less than ten minutes later they were cruising a main street in downtown Boston past large hotels and other buildings. Soon her cabbie let out an exclamation and swerved over in front of the *Benson Hotel* and pulled up behind two other cabs. "Wait here a minute." He jumped out of the cab and ran forward. Dixie watched as he leaned into the passenger side of one of the cabs ahead and spoke to the driver. In a minute he was back, "Yeah, George remembers that fare. He says a tall, blonde skirt with great gams was waiting at the school with a little girl."

Yes! Dixie thought to herself, *now things are moving.* She tried to sound calm as she asked, "Did he remember where he took them?"

The driver nodded, "Sure did."

"Fine. Can you take me there now?" Her driver just smiled and climbed back into the cab. Traffic was getting busier and it took fifteen minutes of fighting traffic before they pulled up on a street filled with industrial businesses; mostly plumbing and electrical contractors. Her driver set the parking brake and looked back at her, "There it is; across the street."

Dixie stared across the street. There was a closed garage door next to a glassed-in office. The sign overhead read: *Bay City Ambulance Company.* She thought for a moment then said with surprise, "It's a private ambulance company." The driver looked back at her, "Isn't this what you were looking for?"

Dixie nodded, "Yes it is." Inside her thoughts were racing. Holding a young girl captive for any length of time would require a good bit of planning. A young girl like that would need constant minding. A private hospital would be a perfect place to stash a captive. Plenty of supervision and no one would ask any questions from a "mother" committing her daughter for private care. She also thought grimly, *What doctor or nurse would believe a young child if she told of being taken from her family? Especially if they had been bought off or told the child was suffering from delusions.*

"Miss? Uh, Miss?"

Dixie's concentration snapped back to the cab driver, "What did you say?"

"I asked if you wanted to go anywhere else."

Dixie reached for the door handle, "Yes, but wait here a moment. I have some questions to ask." She got out of the cab and walked across the street to the ambulance company. Entering she was greeted by an older woman standing behind a counter. Dixie smiled and spoke, "Hello, my name is Jones. I'm trying to locate a patient that was transported by one of your ambulances."

The woman nodded but frowned, "I'm afraid that all of our client files are confidential."

Dixie tried to look helpless, "I'm trying to locate a young girl who I believe you transported. It's important that I locate her."

"Sorry, as I said all client information is confidential." The woman looked suspicious and Dixie could see she would have to try another way.

Dixie nodded as she looked around the office. A corridor led toward the back of the building and a door on the right hand wall probably led to the garage. They were alone and she could hear no other voices. She turned back to the woman taking careful note of her clothing and manner. The woman was middle-aged. Her clothing was clean but inexpensive and Dixie noted a slightly frayed cuff on her blouse. She reached into her purse as she spoke, "May I leave my name for you supervisor. Perhaps he can help me."

The woman was shaking her head as Dixie's hand came out of her purse and laid a five dollar bill on the counter, "It won't do you any good, as I said we don't—" Her voice trailed off as she saw the bill resting under Dixie's fingers. Her mouth was open but closed abruptly. She looked Dixie in the eye and seemed about to speak when Dixie cut her off, "I know this is inconvenient but it's about my niece. She's only eight and I'm afraid I have bad news for her."

The woman seemed really confused now, "Bad news?"

"Yes, my niece has been sick. My sister had her sent to a private hospital last month by one of your ambulances. Now my sister has been in a terrible accident and I have to see my niece to let her know what has happened. It would be wonderful if you could help me." The woman seemed undecided for a minute more before standing up and moving to a file cabinet. She turned and asked, "What was the name?"

Dixie smiled and spoke confidently, "I don't know what name was used. I do know that the ambulance was dispatched on the 17[h] of last month to a private hospital I assume." The counter woman gave Dixie a suspicious look, closed the drawer she had opened and instead pulled a large ledger from beneath the counter. She flipped through the pages then ran her finger down several lines of handwritten script. She spoke, "There was only one ambulance dispatched to a private hospital on that day." She frowned, "Hmmm, there was not a pick up. It seems it left from here." She looked up, confused.

Dixie spoke up, "That's the one. Where did it go?"

"It says here it was dispatched to the *Westfield Sanitarium* in Westfield."

Dixie smiled as she turned to go, "Thank you very much. That's just what I needed to know." As she opened the street door she saw the woman pick up the money on the counter. Hustling back across the street she entered the cab and settled back against the seat back. Her driver leaned over the front seat and asked, "Did you find what you're looking for?"

Dixie nodded, "I certainly did."

He nodded, "Where to now?"

Dixie said, "The *Metrolite Hotel,* and step on it, I've got work to do." As the cab sped off Dixie's mind was racing. First she needed a map to find out where the Westfield was. Then she was going to have to rent a car. The trail was getting warm and Dixie was feeling the thrill of the chase.

• • •

"Handle that thing carefully! It's delicate, and valuable!" The thin man whose name Ronald had learned was Joshua shook his head and watched as Ronald carefully brushed clinging excelsior off the oriental vase. He then carried it across to another man who was repacking them into crates marked "dishware". The second man put it carefully in the crate and fitted a lid to it. He then pasted a shipping address card on the side of the crate. As Ronald turned away to pick up the now empty crate the oriental china had arrived in he caught a glimpse of where the smuggled vases were going to; an address in Atlanta.

It was the next night after Ronald had started building crates marked radios for this new group. The nearly three dozen empty crates stood waiting for their new contents. Joshua had told them a shipment was to arrive soon. Meanwhile several men, including Ronald were re-packing items that had arrived on a merchant ship from the orient that day. Ronald worked hard and didn't talk much to the other men. It had been noticed by Joshua who had given him a positive nod earlier that night. Ronald was pleased. He had passed on a report that day to the *Shrike's* contact and hoped to have more information tomorrow. Meanwhile he kept his head down and his eyes open.

An hour later most of the men were gathered near one of the loading doors. One of the large doors had been rolled up and a large truck backed into the warehouse. When the canvas was flipped back long thin boxes were revealed. With nearly a dozen men working, the truck was quickly unloaded. As soon as it was unloaded, the driver—who had never gotten out of his truck—drove it quickly away into the night. It had been at the warehouse less than ten minutes.

Ronald helped move these battered crates over near the new radio crates they had built the night before. Hammers and pry bars were handed out and the men began tearing the crates open. As the top came off one of the crates Ronald got a good look at its contents. He suddenly understood why the crates they had built were marked radios. He also knew he had important news to report.

• • •

Dixie folded up the road map and set it on the seat next to her. She was getting a later start than she had planned. It was after four when she got back to her hotel the day before; too late to start for Westfield. Instead she had reported by phone that she had tracked the little girl to the cab company and then to the ambulance service. She had promised further reports after she had been to Westfield. She then had dinner and spent the rest of the evening typing up her notes. She had mailed those to herself care of the *New York Bulletin* this morning. After that she rented a car and found a good map of the area. Lastly she had called the long distance operator, gotten a number and been connected with the *Westfield Sanitarium*.

Dixie had learned a lot from speaking with the receptionist at the *Westfield Sanitarium*. She had pretended to be looking for a long-term facility for her aging father. The helpful receptionist had told Dixie that was just what they specialized in; care for recovering patients, long term terminal patients and others who could not take care of themselves. Further prodding had gotten Dixie detailed descriptions of the grounds and facilities as well as reassurances that their "facility was very secure." This had been in response to Dixie's hinting that her father sometimes became disoriented and might wander away. Dixie had responded enthusiastically to the girl's obvious sales pitch and was sure she suspected nothing.

It was late morning as Dixie found the main highway leading west from Boston. She calculated that it would be over an hour to Westfield. The little town was off the highway on lesser traveled roads but she was confident she could be there by noon.

The drive was pleasant. It was a beautiful day in early October. The leaves were starting to change on the trees and the scenery was gorgeous. It was getting quite crisp in the evenings and early mornings but there had not been a frost yet and snow was probably a month off. The highway was fairly well traveled but Dixie made good time. After forty-five minutes of travel she turned off the state highway onto a county road. Going was slower and she almost missed the sign at a turn off reading "Westfield 3 miles". As it was she had to back up before taking the narrow country road to the town.

Less than ten minutes later Dixie was driving down the main street of a picturesque country village. Although she had good directions to the Sanitarium Dixie decided to stop and ask around. Since it was well after noon she decided to have lunch as well. There were only a few cars parked on the street and she had no problem finding a spot directly in front of a local diner.

Inside she sat at the bar to be closer to the waitress. She was greeted by a pleasant-faced young girl and given a menu and a glass of water. Dixie perused the menu and ordered a sandwich and coffee. The only other customers in the place were an older man reading a newspaper while he sipped coffee and a plump looking man who just paying his bill and leaving. As Dixie sipped her coffee she made conversation with the waitress, "Kind of quiet."

The waitress who was busing dishes and picking up her tip looked up at the clock and replied, "You just missed the noon rush. Everyone's gone back to work."

Dixie nodded and sipped, "Good for me, I guess. It shouldn't take long for my sandwich."

The waitress refilled her cup, "Are you in hurry to get back on the road?"

"No, I've got all day actually. I've come to visit my father at the sanitarium."

The waitress nodded knowingly, "Yeah, a lot of their visitors come through here. You certainly picked a nice day to visit. The sanitarium will be pretty I'm sure, what with all the leaves changing." She turned and went into the kitchen returning with Dixie's sandwich. As she set the plate on the counter Dixie questioned, "Have you been there?"

"Sure. It's a pretty place surrounded by trees and very peaceful."

Dixie looked interested, "I guess I never thought to ask; how long has it been here?"

The waitress thought a moment, "Almost two years now."

"I imagine you know a lot of the staff who live here in town?"

"Not really, a couple of the doctors bought houses here but most of the staff live at the sanitarium or live someplace else." She shrugged and wiped

"You just missed the noon rush. Everyone's gone back to work."

the counter. Dixie finished her sandwich and reached for her purse. As she put money on the counter she asked. "I've only been there the one time. Which way do I go again?"

The waitress replied, "Straight up the main street and out of town. At the white church, bear to the right and follow the road about two miles and you're there." Dixie smiled her thanks and added a good tip before heading back to her car. She followed the directions north through town and took the right fork at the church. Sure enough, she soon glimpsed a large white building through the trees on her right. She pulled up at a wide driveway flanked by Brick pillars. Bridging them was a large sign that read *Westfield Sanitarium*. The narrow road continued on.

Dixie pulled up and thought for a moment before she steered her rental car through the gate and up a wide winding driveway. The sanitarium was in fact in a beautiful setting. The two story white building was fairly large. It had a massive center section and a wing branching off to each side. The grounds were nicely landscaped with mature trees scattered across the vast expanse of grass surrounding the building. Dixie pulled her car into the small parking lot at the front of the building. She noticed that a narrow paved driveway continued around to the rear of the building.

She got out and took her time looking over the grounds and building front. Normally in an investigation of this sort Dixie would have done her homework and set up a proper cover story. In this case she might have had some business cards made up and posed as a functionary from the state medical board. With a clipboard, some pointed comments and the proper attitude, she probably could have talked her way in and gotten a good look around. Unfortunately there hadn't been enough time for that. Instead Dixie decided to build on her telephone inquiry. It would at least get her in the door.

Fixing a smile on her face she pushed through the front door and into the cool lobby. It was large and high ceilinged. There were several couches and chairs to her left in a waiting area. To her right was a reception counter manned by a white uniformed nurse. Ahead were a set of twin swinging doors leading deeper into the building. Flanking the swinging doors were hallways leading left and right.

The nurse stood up from behind the low counter and smiled, "May I help you?"

Dixie stepped up to her and smiled confidently back, "Yes. My name is Thompson. I am looking for a place to take care of my father. I was recommended here and I actually spoke to someone earlier today. Could it have been you?"

The young girl shook her head, "I'm afraid not, but I can certainly help you. We're very glad to have clients tour our facility. If you'll wait here I'll see if anyone is available to speak to you." She smiled again as she left through the swinging doors. Dixie immediately made for the right hand corridor. It was wide and well lit. Closed doors ran down each side of the corridor as far as she could see. At the far end of the corridor daylight came though the upper half of a closed door. Immediately to her left a stairwell led upwards. Across from the stairwell there was a door labeled *Women*. Dixie could see numbers on the nearest doors. Each ended in *A*.

Moving quickly to the other corridor Dixie found it to be a mirror image of the first. The only difference was that the door numbers all ended in *B*, and instead of a women's room there was a men's restroom. By the time the nurse returned Dixie was standing near the front door staring innocently out the front window. She turned as a man spoke. He was heavy set, middle-aged man wearing glasses and a white smock, "Are you Mrs. Thompson?"

Dixie held out her hand, "Yes, I am."

The man shook her hand gently and said, "I'm Doctor Jenkins. I'm on staff here. I'll be glad to answer any questions you might have."

The nurse returned to her counter as Dixie spun her story about her elderly father. Doctor Jenkins listened attentively nodding in all the right places as he did. When Dixie finished with, "So I thought I'd drive up and at least look the place over before discussing things with my sisters and our families."

Doctor Jenkins, nodded, "Well, we're a little busy today but I can spare a few minutes to show you around if you'd like."

Dixie nodded enthusiastically, "That would be very nice."

"Good, step this way."

He led her down the hallway past the ladies room and down the hall. He stopped in front of a door numbered *12A*. As he reached for the door knob he spoke, "This room is unoccupied, I believe."

Dixie stepped forward into the room and looked around. It was good sized room with a bed, dresser, wardrobe, two simple chairs and a comfortable armchair near the low sashed window. It was well furnished and Dixie thought to herself that it wouldn't be a bad room for a loved one. She walked across the room so she could look out the window onto the grounds behind the building, "Do all the private rooms have windows?"

The doctor nodded, "Yes. All the client rooms have windows. There is plenty of light and air and as you can see the view from each room is quite pleasant."

Crossing to the door and exiting ahead of the doctor she commented, "It's very nice." As Doctor Jenkins closed the door behind them Dixie
pointed at the knob, "I'm afraid my father is becoming very absent minded.
Sometimes he becomes a little disoriented and tends to wander. Can the
rooms be secured?"

Jenkins looked sympathetic, "Unfortunately we have had more than a
few patients with the same problem. Yes, all doors can be secured if necessary. All staff here carry keys so there is no problem if there is any kind of
emergency." As they walked back to the lobby Jenkins waved at the swinging doors, "Back there we have our treatment rooms including a surgery
and therapy rooms." Walking toward the other wing Dixie noted, "This
looks just like the other wing."

"It is."

Dixie looked up the stairwell, "What's upstairs?"

"There are more patient rooms in each wing. In the center are more
therapy rooms and my and other doctor's offices."

"I'm sure the view over the grounds is better from the second floor. Do
you have rooms available there?"

Yes, we do. Would you care for a look?"

"Yes, thank you." Doctor Jenkins led Dixie to the upper floor. She continued to smile and make appropriate comments as she was shown an almost
identical patient room on the second floor. Meanwhile she was making
mental notes on all she saw. She noted where the elevators were in the center of the building. She took a special interest in the hospital personnel she
saw. Jenkins even showed her through a couple of the treatment rooms on
the second floor. Dixie pretended to be suitably impressed. Twenty minutes later Jenkins was shaking her hand in the lobby and bidding her good
day.

He disappeared into through the swinging doors as the receptionist
spoke, "I hope we've been able to help you Mrs. Thompson."

"Oh, you've all been very helpful. But I wonder if I could use the ladies
room before I go?"

The receptionist nodded, "Of course, its right down there." She pointed
down the right hand hallway. Dixie nodded and made her way quickly
down the hall to the ladies room. Once inside she quickly searched the
bathroom. She looked in both stalls, bending down to look the toilets over
then moved to the porcelain sinks, again bending down to look beneath
them. She then scanned the walls. Finally she went to one of the stalls,
flushed the toilet and then washed her hands noisily in one of the sinks.

She exited the restroom and thanked the receptionist as she turned for the door. Suddenly she turned back and spoke, "Oh, I'm sorry. I forgot to ask Doctor Jenkins about fees. Could I possibly get some written information to take home with me?"

The receptionist turned and hung a clipboard of papers back on a hook behind her and said, "Of course. Let me get you something." She quickly bustled away through the swinging doors.

In a flash Dixie was around the counter and grabbing for the clip board. As she suspected it appeared to be a patient list. There were columns of names, room numbers, admission dates and notes listed for every patient in the institution. Flipping through the pages Dixie didn't waste time looking for names. Undoubtedly Amy Farley would be listed under a false one. Dixie was looking for admission dates. As she ran her finger down column after column she could feel sweat starting on the back of her neck. She tried to keep her breath slow as she continued scanning the entries. There it was! An entry for the correct date; she noted the name and room number and continued on until she was sure there had been no other admissions on that date. As she reached out to hang the clip board back on the wall she heard a voice. She nearly dropped the clip board but got it over the hook and jumped around the counter.

The receptionist pushed through with a several sheets of paper in her hand. Dixie was standing near the counter attempting to look calm. She took the proffered sheets, again thanked the girl and left out the front door. Once outside Dixie looked around. Since she had already established herself as an honest prospective client it certainly wouldn't be suspicious if she looked around the grounds. She turned to her right and walked down a path that paralleled the front of the building.

When she reached the corner she found the end of this wing. It was two stories tall and featureless except for a single door in the middle of the first floor. She drifted toward it and glanced through the window in the upper half of the door. As she suspected she was staring down the length of the main wing. Dixie tried the door but it was locked. As she looked into the hall she saw another stairwell immediately to the right of the door. No doubt it was a fire exit and stairs for emergencies. Dixie nodded to herself and continued around to the rear of the building.

By the time she had circumnavigated the sanitarium and arrived back at her car she had a good idea of the layout of the grounds and building itself. She had passed several patients walking or being pushed around the grounds. She had greeted them cheerfully and been answered back. While doing this she had also noted that exterior lights were scarce around the building. The grounds would not be brightly lit at night. This suited Dixie just fine. It also suited the plan that she had begun to form.

Back in her car she motored slowly back to the village of Westfield. She didn't have to drive far to find what she was looking for. There was a hardware store two blocks down the street from the diner. She took her time there making several purchases of very ordinary items. Satisfied, she paid and stowed her purchases in the trunk of her car. Glancing at her watch she noted that it was after three o'clock. She decided to relax over a cup of coffee and strolled toward the diner. She had several hours to kill before she could return to the Sanitarium.

A few hours later Dixie was sitting in her car waiting. It was after dark. She glanced at her watch. After eight thirty: Time to go. She had coffee in the diner and then ordered some sandwiches to go. Before she had left town Dixie had tried to call the emergency Boston number that she had been given. There had been no answer. She then called New York. The phone had been answered on the first ring by the unknown woman that Dixie was getting used to. She had reported where and how she had located Amy Farley. When told that Dixie was planning a rescue that night, the woman's reply had been clear, "That is not acceptable. Your orders were to observe and report."

Dixie's reply was heavy on sarcasm, "I tried but there was no answer."

The voice tried to mollify her, "Your message will be received soon, until then you are to take no further action."

"Sorry, there's a little girl being held in that place and I'm not letting her stay there another night if I can get her out now."

A pause, "Understood. Your message will be passed on but I cannot tell you when you can expect help."

Dixie couldn't help remarking wryly, "Understood." She hung up shaking her head. This time the Shrike wouldn't be needed. Dixie knew she would be in and out before any of those nurses could even call for help. Besides, she had plans to distract them.

Now Dixie was parked off the road near the Sanitarium. She had checked over her purchases and made the modifications she needed. She had then eaten her sandwiches and waited as the sun sank and the sky darkened. It was time to go. She emptied her purse so she could fit several new items into her large shoulder bag. Ready, she got out of the car and bent down to rub her hands in the loose soil next to the car. She rubbed little bit on one cheek and smeared some on her dress. She couldn't see the results but she was sure she would look the part she was going to act out.

Setting out through the woods she moved in the direction she thought the sanitarium lay; and immediately became disoriented. Not only that, she was continuously tripping over unseen objects on the forest floor. Cursing her stupidity Dixie pulled the new flashlight she had purchased at the hardware store out and used it to make her way forward. It destroyed her night vision but at least kept her from falling on her face every few steps. She kept moving forward periodically turning on the flashlight to look around. After what seem like an eternity, but was probably not more than twenty minutes, she detected lights through the trees. It was off to her left so she changed course accordingly and continued using the flash sparingly.

Finally the trees thinned and Dixie got a look at the sanitarium. She crept slowly up to a large tree at the edge of the lawn surrounding the building. From the building's orientation she had approached the eastern wing. Stowing the flashlight back in her purse Dixie stepped boldly out onto the grass and walked toward the building. It was well lit with many of the patient rooms in the both wings lit behind mostly closed drapes. As she had noted, there relatively few lights scattered around the grounds so it was fairly shadowy until she neared the building.

Dixie worked her way around to the front side paralleling the east wing. Before she reached the well lit parking lot she glanced at her watch. It was just nine o'clock. She took a deep breath and strode toward the main entrance. As she neared the door she sent up a silent prayer that all the day personnel that might recognize her were gone for the day. Reaching the door she yanked on the handle and found it locked. Not too surprising. She leaned forward and peered through the glass as she knocked loudly.

A man in white, short-sleeved uniform was manning the reception counter. At Dixie's knock he looked up from his newspaper in surprise. She sighed in relief; he was a stranger. Seeing Dixie waving through the door he walked across the lobby hefting a ring of keys. Dixie stepped back as he unlocked the door and opened it, "I'm afraid visiting hours are over for tonight."

Dixie stepped up so he could get a good look at her, "Oh, I'm not... uh, actually I need help. My car broke down up the road. I tried to fix it but it was so dark I couldn't see anything under the hood. I really need to use your telephone to call for help." She then gave him her best 'helpless female smile.' It worked. He smiled and held the door wide, "Please come in." Dixie squeezed past him thinking, *So far, so good!*

Once inside, the orderly closed and re-locked the front door and walked back to the reception counter. He reached behind it and pulled a telephone up onto it saying, "I can call the local garage for you. He's probably closed but I'm sure we can reach him at home."

Dixie seemed to think about this for a second, "Does he have a tow truck?"

The orderly looked thoughtful, "Uh, I'm not sure. I suppose he could at least come out and take a look at your car."

Dixie scratched her chin with one dirty finger, "It's pretty dark out there. I wonder what he could accomplish. I do have someone I can call who can get a tow truck out here, although it may take a while. Is it all right if I wait here for him?" She gestured toward a sofa in the waiting area. The orderly seemed to like the idea of a pretty girl keeping him company. He smiled and said, "Of course you can wait here." Dixie came forward and started to reach for the telephone and pretended to notice her hands for the first time, "Oh my! I must be a mess. Is there anywhere I can clean up a bit?" The orderly came forward and gestured toward the east wing hallway, "The ladies room is just down there."

Dixie smiled at him as she moved toward the hallway. Once inside the ladies room she moved immediately into one of the stalls and dropped her purse on the floor. Rummaging in it she came up with a newly purchased adjustable wrench. Reaching under the toilet she quickly twisted the faucet to off. She then went to work on the hose attached to it. Quickly it came loose and Dixie disconnected it. She then turned the faucet back on and water gushed out onto the floor.

Grabbing her purse she quickly repeated the procedure in the second stall. Dixie then dropped her purse near the hall door and hustled to the sinks. Underneath she turned the faucets off and quickly disconnected the hoses. Turning the faucets back on she jumped back to keep from being soaked. Standing near her purse she surveyed her handiwork. Water was rapidly flowing across the tiled floor from the wide open faucets.

Nodding, Dixie stowed the wrench back in her purse and pulled a brown coil from its depths. Unrolling it, she plugged the electrical cord into an outlet near the door and picked up the free end. She had been forced to buy the only two extension cords in the hardware store that afternoon. After cutting off three of the ends and splicing them together she had only about ten feet of cord, but that should be enough. The end Dixie held in her hand had been stripped bare of insulation for several inches and the two copper ends pulled far apart. Plugged in, it was harmless unless something closed the gap between the two copper ends. Standing by the door Dixie waited. Five minutes had passed and the orderly would be expecting Dixie to return but she had to wait until the rapidly growing puddle of water was large enough.

Finally she judged the cord would reach the spreading water. With one hand she reached behind her and opened the door wide and yelled, "Help! Help! There's water everywhere!" She then gently tossed the bare end of the spliced extension cord forward into the water. There was a small "crack!" and a blue white flash and everything went black.

• • •

Just before seven the Shrike bade Farley the ship owner good night and walked to the bus stop on the corner. She rode the bus downtown, appearing to be another worker returning home. Downtown she took a street car to the south side of town where she got off and walked west. This was an area of small businesses, most were closed for the evening.

When she reached the street she wanted she glanced casually around as she walked down the block. She saw no one. Rounding the corner she found the alley behind the block. Working her way carefully down it the Shrike stopped at a metal door. There were words printed in white on it. In the dim light she could barely read: *Bay City Ambulance Co.* Pulling a set of lock picks from her purse the Shrike set to work and in a few minutes had the door unlocked. She slipped inside and closed it behind her.

Once inside a small pocket flashlight illuminated a large garage and three private ambulances. Working her way toward the large roll up doors facing the street the Shrike quickly located a door in a side wall; also locked. Her picks made quick work of this door and the Shrike found herself in the office Dixie had been in the day before. The Shrike wasted no time, she moved directly to the file cabinets behind the counter. Aware that she could be seen if anyone peered through the undraped front window the Shrike used her pocket flash carefully as she searched through the files.

It took nearly ten minutes but finally she found the only file dated the day Amy Farley had been kidnapped and brought here. She quickly stowed it in her purse for perusal later and closed the file drawer. It was quick work to leave the way she had entered, re-locking the doors behind her. She then strolled back to await the next street car. It was nearly an hour long trip back across town but finally, about the time Dixie was working her way through the woods toward the Sanitarium, the Shrike entered her third

Pulling a set of lock picks from her purse the Shrike set to work...

floor room in the nondescript apartment building.

She threw her purse down on the bed, took off her clear glass spectacles and shook her hair out of its tight bun. While she poured herself a drink from a bottle taken from the bottom drawer of her dresser she dialed the long distance operator. When her call was connected she heard the familiar voice, "Report."

"This is Shrike."

"I'm glad you called. Dickson has reported in and may need help."

"Where is she?"

"Westfield, Massachusetts. She established the whereabouts of Amy Farley at the Westfield Sanitarium. Against orders she is attempting a rescue by herself tonight."

The Shrike was annoyed but her voice remained calm as she asked, "What is the time frame?"

"Unknown. She did say she would not be making her attempt until after dinner sometime. I ordered her to phone in as soon as she was successful. If we do not hear anything soon I believe we can assume she has failed."

The Shrike replied, "I will leave for Westfield immediately. If Dickson reports in tell her that I am taking the highway west from Boston and should be in Westfield by"—she looked at her watch—"ten thirty. I will watch for her car along the highway. Anything else?"

"Ronald reported in today. He reports that a very important shipment is being smuggled out in two days on Friday morning's tide by *Southern Star Shipping.*"

"That's good work. Tell him to continue watching but be careful and to stand by for new orders."

"Understood." The Shrike and her contact hung up simultaneously. Then cursing under her breath she began tearing off clothes and changing.

Less than ten minutes later a dark, cloaked figure climbed down the fire escape behind the apartment building and dropped soundlessly into alley. The cloaked figure made its way to the alley entrance and after glancing around carefully made its way down the side street to a battered, dark colored coupe. The coupe started instantly and settled into a low growl. Pulling out quietly the Shrike started across town driving quickly but carefully.

Once she reached the state highway going west the Shrike pulled off the road under a large tree in shadow. She removed her cloak to reveal her dark gray tunic and trousers. Reaching behind the driver's seat she pulled out her long bow and strung it. Replacing it behind the seat she then pulled her shoulder sash out and placed it over head and across her left shoulder. Next she buckled an open top holster with pistol onto her belt so that it was just forward of her left hip, butt forward. Finally she pulled her brown hair back into a ponytail and secured it. Placing her hood on the seat next to her she hopped back into the rumbling roadster, checked traffic, and powered onto the highway. She pressed the accelerator pedal down and effortlessly the little car jumped forward, powering through the night toward Westfield.

. . .

Not looking at the flash Dixie jumped away from the doorway as the lights went out. She knew where the opposite wall would be and had her hands up to catch herself against it. Staying pressed against the wall in the darkness she worked herself toward where she knew the stairwell was. As she did there was a shout followed by a curse from the direction of the reception area. In the dark she could hear the annoyed mumbling of the orderly as he made his blind way down the hallway, "What did that dame do? Owww!" He must have tripped in the dark. Using his cursing as cover Dixie slipped into the dark stairwell and made her way quietly up the stairs.

Already she could hear confused voices echoing down the halls. Knowing that many of the patients here would be ailing or elderly she really wasn't too happy with her diversion but she needed the confusion to allow her to get to Amy's room. Unfortunately, things would probably get worse. Once on the upper floor Dixie pulled a flashlight from her bag and clicked it on to scan the doors for the one she was looking for. The hallway was fast filling with patients who had left their rooms. As she moved Dixie used her, calm, confident voice loudly, "Calm down folks it's just a minor power failure there's nothing to worry about. Please walk down the stairs carefully. Don't run!"

She continued to urge calm as she reached destination: room *18b*. The door was locked. Pulling out a ring of skeleton keys Dixie went to work on the lock. This wasn't the first time she had used them but she didn't make a habit of breaking into buildings so it went slowly. The darkness and confusion didn't help. It took several tries before she found a key that turned the lock and Dixie was sweating by the time she got the door open and herself inside.

Her flashlight beam swept across the room and steadied on a small figure sleeping in the bed. Dixie sat on the edge of the bed and gently shook the young girls' shoulder, "Amy. . . Amy. . . Wake up Amy." Dixie frowned. The child mumbled but remained deeply asleep; her breathing seemed normal but she was out cold. A cold fury swept over the reporter. Those no goods had drugged her! Biting her tongue not to curse, Dixie bundled the girl up in a blanket and picked her up. With her heavy purse over one arm, her arms full of sleeping girl and her flashlight in one hand Dixie was somewhat clumsy as she crossed the room.

The hallway was quieter now. Many patients must have found their way downstairs and out of the building. To her right Dixie could see someone with a flashlight in the other wing giving orders and helping patients. They were working their way toward her. She sighed and flashed her light along the wall. It looked like she would need some additional confusion. The flashlight's beam steadied on a red box bolted to the wall. Walking to it she flashed her light at the stairwell at the end of the corridor and called out loudly, "Everyone please use the stairs! There will be people to help you. Please walk, don't run!" The few people left in the hallway moved toward the stairwell. Glancing the other way Dixie saw that one of the flashlights was moving closer. Shaking her head she turned her flashlight off and used it to smash the glass window on the fire alarm. Tucking the flashlight into the girl's blanket she reached forward and pulled the lever.

Immediately bells began ringing loudly all through the building. Dixie grabbed the flashlight and using it made for the far stairwell. She navigated the stairs as quickly as she could. The lower floor was more crowded. It was still nearly dark, illuminated by a few flashlights near the center of the building. Dixie turned and pushed her way to the door at the end of the corridor. Although locked from the outside it was unlocked inside as she had suspected. She pushed it open, walked outside and held it open with one foot as she waved the flashlight and called, "This way folks! This way! Please exit calmly! This way!" The milling people immediately began moving past her onto the path running around the building. The little girl was starting to get heavy in her arms and Dixie knew she was running out of time. She turned and walked across the lawn toward the dark tree line.

Dixie walked as quickly as she could toward the darkness. She resisted breaking into a run to avoid attention but was still sweating and her breath came in short gasps. She expected any second to hear shouts of pursuit behind her. When she finally reached the first trees she ducked behind one and leaned against it to catch her breath and steady her nerves. After a several seconds she pulled herself together angrily and thought, "I'll bet the Shrike does this kind of thing all the time. If she can do it, so can I." She pushed further into the trees and eventually turning on the flashlight worked her way toward where she hoped the road was.

It took another fifteen minutes for Dixie to stumble out on the narrow country road. It was dark and she was disoriented for a moment. Finally she turned to her left and, praying she had chosen correctly, set off along the road using her flash to scan the trees. Her arm was going numb and she was worried about dropping little Amy when she finally saw the blue of her rented car through the trees. Gratefully she wrenched open the passenger side door and lowered the girl to the passenger seat. Throwing her heavy purse in the back seat she slid tiredly behind the wheel. She started the car, turned on her lights and pulled out onto the road driving toward Westfield.

• • •

In a darkened office two men dressed in white stood over a desk illuminated by the flashlights they held. The shorter one was complaining loudly, "She's gone?"

The other replied, "We're still looking but her room is empty and we can't find her anywhere."

"You've done a count?"

"Yeah, all the other patients are accounted for."

The shorter one was thoughtful for a moment, "Her door was locked. That means someone who knew where she was and got her out." He spoke sharply, "Has anyone been asking for her or any young child?"

The taller one said, "No. But there was a skirt here today looking around."

"Hmmm, what was her name?"

"Don't know. Dr. Jenkins was showed her around. I think she was looking for a place for a relative."

"Huh." He scratched his chin thoughtfully, "There haven't been any visitors around here except relatives for a couple of weeks. What did this woman look like?"

"Uh, blonde, sorta; I only saw her from a distance. I did see her get into her car as she was driving away."

"Yeah, what was she driving?"

"A blue Chevy."

The shorter nodded and lifted the receiver of the desk phone. As he dialed the taller man asked, "You calling them?"

"That's what we're paid to do." There was pause as he waited. Then he spoke, "This is Jamison at the sanitarium. There's been a problem with your...package." A pause, "Yes, I'm afraid its missing but we may have a clue for you—"

• • •

Dixie pulled up in front of the diner where she had eaten earlier. Leaving the still sleeping girl in the passenger seat she hurried inside. On the way she stopped and stared at a commotion down the street. There were lights and a lot of activity around the fire station. Men in civilian clothes were running toward the building while cars were pulling up in front. She grimaced and pulled the diner door open. Inside she smiled at a different waitress than had served her earlier and ordered a cup of coffee before heading for the phone booth in the rear corner. Once inside, it took a minute to be connected and the now familiar female voice to answer, "Report."

"This is Dickson. I have the girl. I'm now heading back to Boston."

"Is the girl hurt?"

"No."

"Where are you calling from?"

Dixie looked out at the diner as the only other patron, an older man, paid and left, "I'm calling from Westfield at the diner."

The unknown woman digested this for a moment, "Be aware that the Shrike is aware of your rescue attempt and is even now traveling west toward you. Keep a lookout for her on the highway. Is there any sign of pursuit?"

"No. I think they're all still busy at the sanitarium."

"Proceed toward Boston. Stay on the main highway. If you do not meet the Shrike on the road, take the girl to your hotel and await further instructions. Be careful."

Dixie smiled, "Thanks, I'll be in Boston in an hour or so." There was a click and the line went dead. She hung up and walked back to the counter where her coffee was waiting. She slipped onto a stool and glanced out the window where she could clearly see her car. A siren sounded in the street getting louder until a fire engine swept by headed out of town. Still holding the coffee cup she asked the waitress, "What's all the excitement?"

The girl shrugged, "Fire alarm sounded a few minutes ago. Don't know where the fire's at."

"Kind of slow aren't they?"

The girl shrugged again, "Its volunteer unit. Everybody comes from home this time of night. Dixie sipped as two more cars flew past the diner in the direction the engine had gone. As Dixie stood up and reached for some change the waitress asked, "Lost?"

Dixie put a dime and a nickel on the counter and smile as she turned for the door, "No, just headed back to Boston. Thanks for the coffee." Back in the car Dixie drove slowly down the street. There were a few more lights on and she saw one person looking out a window but otherwise Westfield was still quiet.

It took a while to get to the highway. Dixie missed a turn on the dark road and had to backtrack but twenty minutes later she was turning left onto the highway toward Boston.

• • •

Fifteen minutes after Dixie left Westfield a dark sedan drove into Westfield and stopped at a stop sign. It paused a moment and then pulled up in front of the only business that seemed open: the diner. A man in an over coat got out leaving the motor running and entered the diner. He was dark and thin. His hat was pulled low and the waitress couldn't see the hard look in his eyes as she asked him if he wanted a cup of coffee. He shook his head and said, "I'm looking for a friend who might have passed by here; a blonde woman driving a blue Chevy."

The waitress nodded as she chewed her gum, "Sure, she just left."

"Did she say where she was going?"

Yeah, Boston, said she was headed home."

"How long ago?"

The waitress shrugged, "Ten or fifteen minutes ago." The man nodded and left. Back in the car he put it in gear and drove out of town. As he did he spoke to the two other men in the car, "She's headed for Boston. We're behind but we can catch her on the road. He pressed down on the accelerator and the powerful car shot ahead toward the highway.

• • •

Having made it to the highway unharmed, Dixie breathed easier. She even smiled to herself. She wasn't used to this kind of thing but had brought off the rescue pretty neatly. And she hadn't needed any help. She hummed to herself as she glanced at the still sleeping form next to her.

She made pretty good time at first. It was after ten o'clock and traffic was fairly light. Except for a few large trucks she saw few other autos. Soon though, she caught up to a large, slow moving truck and trailer. She slowed behind it and looked for a chance to pass. Unfortunately the highway had no stretch straight enough to pass safely. She waited patiently. There was no pursuit and she knew the Shrike was somewhere on the road headed toward her. She peered carefully at every approaching car that passed, expecting to see the battered coupe that the Shrike drove.

Soon headlights appeared in her mirror. They approached quickly and then slowed as they caught up. Dixie shrugged impatiently. Hopefully this truck would see that traffic was backing up behind him and pull over soon. After another few miles the truck slowed and signaled. Dixie slowed almost to a stop as the truck turned off onto a side road. Once clear she sped up. The car behind her sped up also.

As the two cars rounded a turn the sedan behind Dixie pulled into the oncoming lane and accelerated up next to her. The straight stretch they were on wasn't very long and Dixie tapped the brakes, shaking her head at the other driver's poor judgment. To her surprise the other car did not speed past her. Instead it slowed just ahead of her and swerved toward her rented car.

Dixie jabbed the brakes hard and swerved toward the shoulder. Dirt and gravel flew up against the under carriage as her right wheels hit the shoulder. "Hey, what are you doing?" she yelled as if the other driver could hear. She wrenched the wheel to the left and got back onto the highway. The other car stayed in the lane next to her as they sped around a slight bend. Her mind raced as she tried to get a glimpse of the crazy driver of the sedan.

Dixie accelerated trying to get ahead of the sedan but it was powerful and maintained its position next to her. The unknown driver suddenly jerked his car toward her again. Dixie couldn't react fast enough and sparks flew as the heavier vehicle scraped along the left fender of the rented car. Dixie swore and stabbed the brakes. Her tires screeched and suddenly she was behind the sedan. The two cars swept into a long straight stretch. The sedan braked and swerved into the other lane. Off her left front it then cut sharply directly for Dixie's left front bumper. It hit with a clang and Dixie fought for control as she was pushed toward the shoulder.

The right front tire dropped off into the gravel as Dixie fought for control. The ground sloped and suddenly she was bouncing through dirt and high grass along the shoulder of the road. A small sapling appeared in her headlights and she took it off at the ground without even slowing, the branches making a terrible racket as she drove over it. She braked as dust and debris obscured her vision. The car bumped over something hard with a bang, bouncing Dixie's head against the padded roof. She reflexively stabbed the brake pedal hard and shot out a hand to steady the blanket wrapped figure next to her. The car skidded over loose leaves and grass and came to a stop in a cloud of dust. The deceleration caused Dixie's hat to fly

Dixie fought for control as she was pushed toward the shoulder.

off just before her forehead painfully hit the steering wheel.

Shaking her head Dixie shoved her door open. The sinister sedan was stopped over a hundred feet ahead. Quickly it shifted into reverse and backed toward her. Shaking off her dizziness, Dixie leaned into the car, and pulled the girl into her arms. The pursuing sedan had swerved over to the shoulder and came to a stop forty feet ahead of Dixie's car. As she turned to run, she saw the glare of oncoming lights from over a slight rise two hundred yards down the road toward Boston. She ran across the road as three men jumped from the car; all with guns in their hands. Dixie was in the middle of the road running toward a fence line on the other side when the oncoming vehicle topped the rise and the scene was thrown into stark relief by its headlights. She looked over her shoulder as she ran and saw a small auto steering directly for the armed men in the road. They turned but did not have time to shoot before the car was on them. The men threw themselves in all directions, reminding Dixie of pins in a bowling alley hit by a bowling ball.

The car immediately braked hard and turned, sliding sideways in the road. It skidded past Dixie as she reached the other side of the road and threw herself down in the grass. She protected the blanket wrapped girl as she hit the ground but kept her head up to watch developments…she had recognized that car. The dark coupe came to rest sideways in the middle of the road amid a smelly cloud of burnt rubber. It was perhaps forty feet off to Dixie's right. To her left over fifty feet away, the three men were getting to their feet. One was swearing loudly. Another yelled, "Get the kid!"

As this was happening the coupe's driver's door flew open and a dark clad figure dove onto the pavement. Dixie watched in admiration as the figure rolled over twice and came up to one knee gracefully as if she had practiced the maneuver all week. Like lightning the Shrike drew an automatic pistol from her waist and began firing. Gunfire answered from down the road. It was dark on the road with the various cars' headlights pointing off in all the wrong directions but so many bullets were flying that Dixie could easily follow the action by the flashes of the guns.

Ignoring incoming fire the Shrike was quickly firing aimed shots one after another. *Bang! Bang! Bang! Bang!* One of the gunmen dropped his gun and staggered back. The Shrike kept firing. Dixie had thought she was using a .45 but the masked figure did not stop to reload. She watched in amazement as the Shrike kept firing without let up. Driven back by the continuous fire the two remaining gunmen were retreating toward their car reloading as they went. The wounded man staggered with them.

Finally the Shrike stood up. Something dropped from her pistol and the Shrike called out loudly but calmly to Dixie, "Get in the car." As Dixie stood up to run for the coupe, the Shrike shoved another magazine into her pistol and began firing again. Rounding the rear of the coupe Dixie felt and heard the little car vibrate as it was hit by flying lead. She kept her head down as she scrambled into the coupe while thinking, *She must have fired a dozen shots without reloading. What kind of gun is that?*

Reaching their sedan, the wounded man collapsed as he was trying to climb into the back seat. Another helped him as the third fired his reloaded revolver twice more and jumped behind the wheel. The Shrike was standing up now holding that improbable pistol in both hands as she started firing again. The range was long but Dixie heard metallic bangs and glass shattering as bullets thudded into the big sedan. She stayed low in the coupe clutching the blanket wrapped girl to her chest watching as the last gunman turned and fired off a parting shot at the Shrike. That was a mistake. His gun flew out of his hand as he was hit in the shoulder by one of the Shrike's well aimed shots. Clutching it, he turned and tumbled into the open door of the sedan on top of his badly wounded pal. The sedan then shot off down the highway in a cloud of dust, the rear door swinging back and forth.

Dixie lifted her head and looked around. It was suddenly quiet after the crash of gunfire. The Shrike holstered her gun and walked toward the coupe. Sliding behind the wheel she asked without looking, "Are you two all right?"

Dixie answered as the Shrike put the coupe in gear and swung it toward her mired car, "Yes, we're okay."

The Shrike pulled up behind the now battered rental car and looked at the girl in Dixie's arms, "Why isn't she awake? No one could sleep through that racket!"

Dixie stroked the sleeping girl's forehead gently as she answered, "Those no goods at the sanitarium had her drugged. She'll be okay but she's still sleeping solidly."

The Shrike was looking in the rear view mirror as she replied, "Perhaps it's just as well." Dixie could see the Shrike's gray mask illuminated in reflected light, the wide black stripe standing out clearly, and realized there were headlights approaching from the rear. The Shrike sank down in the seat and said, "Duck." Seconds later a large truck roared past heading toward Boston. When she sat up the Shrike opened her door and got out, she leaned back in and asked, "Can your car be driven?"

Dixie replied, "I think so but it's stuck in loose dirt. We might be able to push it free."

The Shrike shook her head, "No time. Get anything out of it you want and lock it up. We'll send someone to tow it back to town tomorrow. Right now we have to go." Dixie laid the girl on the seat and walked rather shakily toward her car. Now that the shooting was over she was feeling a little weak kneed. As she grabbed her hat and purse out of the car she saw the Shrike in the road picking up the gun dropped by the unknown gunman.

Back in the car Dixie picked up the little girl and got settled as the Shrike shoved the coupe into gear. Gravel spun from beneath the rear wheels as she revved the car hard. Once on the road she pushed the little car up to a breakneck speed. "What's the hurry?" Dixie asked.

Concentrating on the road the Shrike answered, "When those men report in, our enemy's next step will be to grab Farley. We have to get there first and get him and his daughter to safety. I didn't want to rush; I had hoped to plan this rescue a little better." Dixie's face flushed in the dark interior of the car and she decided to change the subject, "Say, I've got to know. What kind of crazy gun is that you're using? How the heck can it fire that many times?"

There was a slight pause before the Shrike replied, "It's kind of rare; made in Belgium. You don't see many of them here in America...I need to concentrate now." Dixie shut up as the Shrike swerved around the truck that had recently passed them. She kept the rest of her questions to herself as they rocketed toward Boston.

A half hour later they were slowing carefully as they entered the built up area of the city. Dixie thought to herself wryly that it might be hard to explain the mask and guns to a traffic cop if they got stopped. It was nearly midnight and traffic was light as they drove through town. It was dark and peaceful as they turned into the quiet neighborhood of homes near the Farley house.

The Shrike killed the coupe's lights and they drifted to the curb two houses past the Farley residence. They got out, closing their doors quietly and the Shrike led them down the sidewalk, then up to the front door of the house. Dixie wasn't too surprised when the Shrike produced a key and unlocked the front door; curious but not surprised. They entered house and the Shrike produced a pocket flashlight and led the way up the stairs. They were just in time, Dixie thought, because little Amy was beginning to stir. Once on the second floor the Shrike pointed to a door and whispered, "I'll turn on the light. You go in first." She opened the door wide and reached around the door frame and flipped on the overhead light. Dixie stepped forward and entered the room.

The startled Farley was shielding his eyes as he sat up in bed, "Who are you? What is …Amy! My god!" The ship owner threw back the bed covers and jumped forward as Dixie held out Amy to him. He grabbed his daughter and hugged her to his chest. He was crying. Dixie didn't know whether to cry herself or slip quietly out into the darkened hallway. The Shrike made the decision for her. She stepped forward into the room and said quietly, "Mr. Farley."

His eyes were closed and he must not have heard because she repeated, "Mr. Farley."

He opened his eyes and was certainly startled. He took a step back and his mouth opened to yell. As he did the Shrike stepped back and held up both gloved, empty hands, "Calm down sir. We don't mean you any harm. We're actually here to help you." The frightened man looked from the Shrike to Dixie and back again. Dixie smiled disarmingly hoping it would help.

"But Amy, how…why?"

The Shrike spoke calmly, "We rescued her from her captors. We know unknown men kidnapped her and are forcing you to do as they say. They're using your ships and warehouses to smuggle goods in and out of the country."

Farley's face had gone still, then pale and now it sagged with shock. He whispered, "How could you know that?"

The masked figure replied, "I know a lot. What I don't know is who is behind this smuggling ring. Do you know?"

The man shook his head, "I don't know. All instructions came over the phone, always here at home and at night. I…I didn't want to do what he said but they had Amy. I didn't know what to do. I couldn't even tell my wife. Thank God she's been visiting relatives…Thank you for bringing her back to me." He again hugged the now stirring little girl.

The Shrike nodded, "No one would have done anything different, but I'm afraid you're still in danger. We have to get you and your daughter to safety right now. The men who took your daughter know we rescued her and they know where you live. They could be on their way right now."

Farley tuned pale again, "All right. What should I do?"

"You need to get packed, take one suitcase. Hurry!" The Shrike turned and motioned Dixie out into the hall "I need you to pack a suitcase for the girl. Her room is there," he pointed across the hall. "And the suitcases are in that closet." Dixie went to the closet and pulled out two suitcases.

The Shrike picked up the phone in the hall and started dialing. Dixie carried one suitcase into Farley's bedroom. He had laid Amy on the bed and was pulling clothes out of his dresser. Dixie then crossed to Amy's room, turned on the light and started packing some clothes for her. As she did she marveled at the depth of the Shrike's knowledge. She not only had a key to the Farley's house but knew the layout as well. A sudden thought came to her; *Just how many people does she have working for her, watching and sneaking around?* As she added a couple of small toys to the suitcase before closing it, she decided the Shrike was not just mysterious but a little scary as well.

She turned and re-entered Farley's bedroom. He was now dressed and was just adding some last items to his suitcase. He was asking the Shrike, "So you won't tell me who you really are?"

The Shrike shook her head, "The Shrike will do for now."

He closed the suitcase and looked up, "What kind of name is that?"

The Shrike said firmly, "It's not a name but it's what some people have come to call me. All you need to know is that I intend to stop the men who have threatened your family. Are you ready?" As she spoke Dixie peered at the gun holstered at her waist. At first glance it looked like a Colt .45 but as she stared she could see that the butt was much larger and more square shaped. The magazine in the butt was also wider and the gun had handsome hardwood grips. She hadn't seen anything quite like it. Her attention snapped back to the Shrike as she asked Farley, "Are you ready?" He nodded.

The Shrike brushed past Dixie flipping off the light as he went. "Wait inside," she whispered. She slipped quietly down the stairs and carefully opened the front door a crack to peer outside. Dixie moved to the bed and picked up the second suitcase. With Farley carrying Amy, who was mumbling sleepily, they went down the stairs and waited at the front door. Moments later the Shrike whispered, "I've called a taxi, Mr. Farley. It will be here soon. You should go directly to the train station. Get tickets and go to your wife. When you get there tomorrow explain what has happened. Then all three of you have to go into hiding for a while."

Farley asked, "For how long?"

The Shrike chuckled under her mask and looked toward Dixie, "Watch the New York newspapers. They should break big news on the smuggling ring soon. Stay here while I look around." She then slipped out the front door. A few minutes later she was back and swung the door open. She motioned them to wait on the darkened porch and spoke, "It looks quiet.

When the taxi arrives take it directly to the train station, Mr. Farley. We will follow you in our car." Farley nodded. The Shrike must have visited her car because she was now wearing a long dark cloak with the hood up to conceal her face.

Soon a taxi pulled to a stop in front of the house. The Shrike motioned everyone forward with an arm. She led; her hand on her gun. Farley and his daughter followed with Dixie last, carrying the suitcases. They quickly bundled everything into the taxi. The Shrike faded back out of the way while Dixie gave orders to the cabbie. It pulled away safely and the two women hustled to the coupe and pulled out after it. As they followed the cab through the quiet streets the Shrike gave Dixie new orders, "Miss Dickson, you will go into the station and make sure they get their tickets and are safe. I will circle the station until you return. After that we will go to my room." Dixie murmured her assent.

Once at the station Dixie hopped out and followed Farley inside. She loitered nearby watching as they bought tickets. Once they were settled in the well-lit waiting area, she hustled back outside. In the bright light of the station she had seen the mess her clothes were in. They were dusty, her stockings were run and her shoes were scuffed. She looked like she'd been through a battle which was actually fairly accurate. Outside she had to wait for a couple of minutes until the battered coupe pulled up. Dixie hopped quickly in and they were away.

Minutes later they pulled up in front of the Shrike's building. The Shrike turned to her, "Your actions were ill advised, Miss Dickson. Things could have gone badly." She paused and Dixie nodded but held her tongue. "Still everything came out fairly well. Our hand has been shown, though, and we must move quickly. You're needed back in New York. You will drive this car." She handed Dixie the keys and a slip of paper, "Leave the car locked at this location with the keys under the seat. You will be contacted with further orders."

"But what will you do?"

"I have made other arrangements. Good luck." She got out of the car, reached behind the seat and pulled what looked like a strung bow from behind it. Turning she walked away. By the time Dixie got out of the car the Shrike had faded into the shadows. Dixie shook her head and got behind the wheel and drove slowly away.

• • •

The Shrike entered her room via the fire escape. Once inside she quickly changed into fashionable attire and packed her clothes and gear into two suitcases. Her bow went into a long thin case that contained a second bow. She then called a taxi. Her room was paid ahead and she locked the door before leaving and waiting on the sidewalk for her cab. When the cab arrived the Shrike got in and ordered, "Jeffery Field, cabbie." He looked surprised but shrugged and dropped the flag. The field was east of town but traffic was light and they made good time. Shortly after one in the morning they turned into the airfield parking lot. The Shrike ordered the cabbie to bypass the terminal and drive around to the private flight line.

He complied and pulled up at a four foot high chain link fence next to a line of small hangars. The Shrike paid the cabbie and carried her bags through a gate out to the wide paved apron. Thirty yards away a white and red trimmed aircraft was idling, its powerful radial engine ticking over loudly. As the Shrike watched, a man in leather jacket stood up in the hatch over the cockpit. Seeing her he waved and disappeared inside. A moment later he opened a door in the side of the aircraft and dropped to the ground. He trotted over to the Shrike and smiled, it's good to see you Mrs. Walker."

The Shrike smiled and reached out her hand and drawled, "It's good of y'all to come out this late."

The young pilot shook his head, "You're paying me well, ma'am. I've been waiting to hear from you. The *Lady Hawke* is all fueled up and ready to go. We can take off as soon as you're aboard."

"Fine. Ah need to be in Philadelphia as soon as possible."

"Then let's go." He grabbed up her two bags and turned toward the aircraft. After stowing all of her bags in the aft compartment he offered his hand to the Shrike who took it with a smile as she climbed into the cabin. It was well appointed with seats for five. Noting that the woman immediately began to buckle her seat belt, the pilot turned and climbed through a hatch into the cockpit. He looked back as he buckled his own belt and yelled over the engine roar, "We'll have you in Philly in time for an early breakfast, Mrs. Walker." He then reached behind him into the passenger compartment and swung the cockpit door shut. It was padded on its inner side and became his back rest when closed.

The Shrike sat back patiently as they taxied out to the runway. They immediately swung on to it and accelerated quickly. Soon they were off the ground and the pilot had put them into a climb. The Shrike reached for her large purse. Pulling out a file she began to read as the aircraft droned into the night

• • •

Dixie drove through the night to New York. Once there she dropped the Shrike's car where directed and took a cab home to her modest apartment. She had been gone three whirlwind days and was exhausted. She needed sleep.

She slept until afternoon. Rising, she showered, dressed and made it in to the paper by three o'clock. Several other reporters inquired about her health as she crossed the city room. She had called in sick before setting out for Boston. Dixie started going through her mail to catch up on things. As she read a copy boy ran up bearing an envelope, "For you Miss Dickson."

Dixie opened it and found a note from the Shrike. She glanced rather guiltily around and read quickly. The letter contained new instructions for her. She thought a moment and reached for the telephone. There was work to be done.

• • •

Two nights later the Philadelphia docks were still busy at eleven o'clock at night. Ships were being loaded or unloaded and trucks came and went. Yet not every warehouse was active and there were many darkened buildings and pools of shadow between them. The Shrike, dressed in gray, a bow in one hand, stood against the wall of a darkened warehouse almost invisible in the shadows. A large figure entered from a lighted street and crept toward her. She stepped out from the wall and queried, "How did it go?"

Ronald answered from the darkness, "I made the calls. The customs guy seemed more receptive than the FBI agent but I think I convinced them both."

"The time?"

"I told them things would be over by midnight and they better get here quick."

The Shrike nodded, "There won't be any problem with you being late?"

"No there's no set time and we're supposed to work until dawn. The *Santa Catalina* sails on the morning tide; about seven thirty."

"All right, it's after eleven. Go to your job. Work hard. The only thing you have to do is make sure the front door is unlocked. Will that be difficult?"

"I don't think so. There is a usually a lot going on. I should be able to slip over to the door and unlock it without anyone paying attention to me."

"Good. When the authorities pull up we'll hear them. Make for the back door. I'll be watching from above. I'll cover you if anyone tries to stop you. There are lots of shadows on the piers. If you have to, you can always use the water. I'll meet you back at the car."

"But how will you get away?"

"Over the roof the same way I got in. I may not even be seen in the shadows of the rafters. I am here just to eliminate the lookout and to cover you if things go wrong."

Ronald nodded, "Good luck Shrike." Then he turned back toward the front of the warehouse row.

"Good luck to you," the Shrike murmured as she turned the other way.

At the rear corner of the warehouse the Shrike found a metal ladder that ran up the side of the tall building. Climbing it nimbly, she was on the flat roof in seconds. She moved carefully around ventilators and skylights to the front of the warehouse and carefully looked over the edge of the roof. She stood atop Warehouse 11. Her target was two buildings down. The street in front was wide and ran north and south for hundreds of yards along this row of warehouses. She had reconnoitered the dock earlier that day. She hadn't been able to climb to the roof of a warehouse but she had gotten a look inside one and had a plan. The warehouses were nearly identical. Front and rear doors in each, but more importantly they were all the same height and all had skylights.

The Shrike turned and ran lightly across the warehouse to the other side. There were some people loading crates onto a truck between the two buildings, working by spotlights. This wasn't a problem. The Shrike moved to a heavy metal pipe that protruded from the roof near the side of the building. It was hollow, about three feet tall with a head angled toward the next building. From it a heavy cable ran into the darkness across the alley.

The Shrike grabbed the cable with one hand and vaulted to the top of the pipe. She balanced atop it easily and reached a foot carefully forward onto the cable. It gave a bit under her weight as she tested it. She slowly extended her five foot long bow, held in both hands horizontally in front of her. As she stepped forward onto the cable she absently thought to herself that it had more sag than she was used to but on the plus side it was much wider. Keeping herself upright the Shrike carefully and deliberately walked across the cable. Ten cautious steps later she had reached a corresponding pipe on the next building and hopped down lightly.

Crossing to the other side she could look across at the warehouse she was interested in. As she climbed to the top of a similar pipe near the edge of the roof she could see the skylights of the warehouse across from her were dimly lit. The smugglers were hard at work; hopefully Ronald was there unsuspected among them. The Shrike stepped out confidently on the cable and walked meticulously across it. She shifted the bow slightly to the left and then right to maintain her balance as she walked calmly across the darkened gap, not looking or even thinking about the thirty foot drop to the concrete.

Reaching the other side the Shrike dropped quietly down and into a crouch. Looking around she made out a figure standing on the front side of the warehouse staring down into the street. Standing up, she glided silently across the roof of the warehouse toward the lookout. As she neared him she smelled tobacco smoke. She was about twenty feet away from the rough clothed figure when he threw a cigarette butt into the street and turned toward her.

The figure took a step and froze as it saw the dark garbed figure. She strode quickly forward. The man reached for a pocket and lunged toward her. He had a wicked looking knife in his hand as he reached the Shrike but never got a chance to use it. A booted foot came up in a kick and sent the knife spinning across the roof top. Swearing, the man pushed in swinging his fists wildly. The Shrike blocked his right with her bow but his left caught her a sharp blow on the shoulder. She stepped back and dropped to the roof of the warehouse, her leg sweeping out hard to strike the back of the man's ankles. His feet swept out from under him, the lookout went down with a thud. He attempted to get to his knees but one of the Shrike's soft boots connected with his ribs. Momentarily stunned he was helpless as the Shrike leaped on his back and finished him with the edge of a stiffened gloved hand to the back of his neck.

The Shrike quickly stripped the man of his belt and used it to bind his hands behind him. Then she gagged him with a handkerchief pulled from her sash. She located his dropped knife and set off across the dim warehouse roof. She paused to look down into a rather dusty skylight. The warehouse was fairly well lit from hooded lights hung from unseen rafters about twenty feet above the floor. The area above the lights was in deep shadow. The Shrike moved to another skylight that was more centrally located. She tossed the guard's knife into the darkness and searched for a latch.

Locating it, she slowly lifted the glass frame and stuck her head into the building. Above the level of the lights was about eight feet of darkness to the roof. This area was crisscrossed by a network of metal pipes, catwalks and a network of metal rafters that supported the roof. Scattered about the warehouse, steel I-beams ran from floor to ceiling with the metal rafters connecting them. A wide metal frame ran between two I beam pillars about four feet to her right. Directly below her a one-inch diameter pipe ran parallel to the metal frame.

His feet swept out from under him the lookout went down with a thud.

The Shrike unstrung her bow and quickly unscrewed the five foot long bow into two sections. She slid the two halves into a sheath on her back. She then climbed over the ledge supporting herself on the skylight frame with one hand. She lowered herself carefully until the backs of her knuckles rested on the frame. She could feel the pipe against her legs. Taking a breath she let go of the skylight frame and dropped four feet, her hands deftly grabbing the pipe. She hung there swinging slightly and then swapped hands until she faced the opposite way. Slowly she started pumping her legs back and forth. Soon her legs were swinging up high in front and behind her as she swung from the pipe. On a final swing when her feet were at their apex in front the shrike let go of the pipe and flew forward. She landed deftly on the metal beam with barely a sound.

Kneeling down, the Shrike scanned the warehouse floor below. She was over twenty feet in the air. To her left were the large roll up doors, all closed, and a smaller door at the right front corner. To her right on the dock side the set up was the same. Certain lights suspended from chains illuminated islands of light where men were busy building and loading wooden crates. The corners of the warehouse were shadowy. She could see Ronald ahead and to her left busy wielding a hammer on a new crate.

Rising, she turned and walked the narrow beam twenty feet to another metal I-beam and looked below. In the light men were busy taking rifles out of long thin cases and placing them into the new crates that they had just built. She nodded. It was as Ronald said; a large shipment of what appeared to be surplus weapons were being smuggled out of the country. Ronald had told her the weapons were supposedly headed for Spain via Mexico and Cuba.

Glancing at her watch she saw that it was nearly eleven thirty. The Shrike glided along the beam to an upright support closer to the front door. She knelt down again and un-knotted the cord holding her arrows in their case. She carefully pulled out a metal shaft and laid it on the beam in front of her. The shaft was about an inch wide behind the sharp head for about eight inches before narrowing back to a 3/8" shaft running to the feathers. She thought for a moment and placed another identical arrow next to it. Then she pulled the two halves of her bow out and quickly assembled them. She was just stringing it when she noticed Ronald below her look around and edge toward the door in the front corner of the warehouse. He was nearing it when a voice stopped him, "Hey Sam! Where you going?"

Turning and jerking a thumb over his shoulder Ronald answered back, "Just gonna take a quick smoke."

"Take it later. I need a hand over here."

Ronald shrugged and walked toward the man standing somewhere beneath the Shrike. Muttering something about luck, she reached into her sheath and pulled another arrow out. It had a blunt tip that widened out into a two inch long, one and half inch wide cylinder attached to the long shaft. She laid it carefully on the beam alongside the other arrows. She picked one of the first two arrows and fitted it to the bow string then froze in place, her head cocked, listening carefully.

A moment later she heard powerful engines coming rapidly closer. She pulled the string back, aimed downwards and let fly. Less than a second later the arrow impacted on a vertical support beam perhaps eight feet up from the floor. There was a flash and the arrow fell to the concrete floor burning with a light so brilliant that it could not be looked at directly.

Ignoring the screams, shouts and curses coming from below the Shrike picked up the blunter shaped arrow and nocked it in her bow. Now she could hear brakes screeching and car doors slamming in front of the warehouse. Shifting her aim the Shrike aimed toward the corner of the building. The range was perhaps seventy feet but she did not hesitate and let fly toward the small door. The arrow impacted just above the door knob. There was another flash simultaneous with a loud bang that echoed across the large open space. The door slammed open against the wall and sagged on its hinges. Grabbing up the third arrow the Shrike aimed at another vertical beam on the other side of the warehouse. She again let fly as loud shouts came from the front of the building, "Hands up, FBI!" The arrow impacted and, like the first one, the magnesium along with the aluminum shaft burned glaringly bright.

There was chaos everywhere. Armed officers were pouring through the shattered front door. They were shouting and brandishing guns. Below, the smugglers ran in all directions like cockroaches in the light. Several of them had pulled out handguns and began firing wildly. The police answered and the bullets flew. The Shrike decided that her work was done. She turned and ran along the beam.

Some of the shots were directed upwards. After the second arrow, someone had spotted the gray garbed figure in the overheard shadows and shouted her location. Shots flew past. The Shrike was still above the glare of the lights and her movements were in deep shadow. She looped her bow over her head and one shoulder and ran lightly along the beam towards the skylight she had entered through.

As she did, a single wild shot hit the right heel of her soft boots as she raised it to take a step. She felt a stab of pain that threw her off balance. Knowing she could not retain her balance the Shrike pushed off the beam with her left foot. Arching outward she reached for a hanging light and grabbed the supporting chain as she fell. Her gloved hands got a firm hold as her momentum took her outward in a long arc. She got a wild view of the warehouse as she swung. There was still shooting and people were yelling and cursing.

Reaching the apex of her forward arc the chain paused for an instant before swinging back. The Shrike pulled her legs up on the back swing and jackknifed them forward as she swung ahead. This increased her swing and at the forward apex she let go. Her body arced forward in the dim overhead space and she grabbed a water pipe running the width of the building. She let her swing ease a bit and then used the remaining momentum to lift herself waist high on the pipe. She swung a leg over it and straddled the pipe. She then quickly boosted herself to her feet, grabbed a roof brace and walked a few feet forward along the pipe to a skylight. In seconds she was pulling herself on to the flat roof of the warehouse.

Favoring her stinging heel the Shrike hustled to the rear roof. There were flashlights and shouts from below. She could see a plainclothes officer handcuffing a roughly dressed dockworker. Another held a light and gun. Reaching into the bandolier running across her chest she pulled a cylindrical object from it. She pulled a pin from the grenade and dropped it over the edge. Another grenade followed the first. They both went off as they hit, spewing clouds of gray smoke. At the top of the ladder the Shrike grasped the uprights and pressing her feet against them slid quickly down. She dropped off into the cloud of the smoke. There were voices all around her and she knew that she had only seconds to make her escape. Turning, she raced in what she though was the right direction.

Almost instantly she ran into a solid object that cursed as she bounced off it. The Shrike ducked and threw out an elbow that connected with something and dashed forward through the smoke. She came out of it and ducked behind a stack of barrels. There were more shouts but no one seemed to know exactly where she had gone. Keeping low, the dark garbed figure disappeared into the shadows.

Ten minutes later she was opening the rear door of a maroon-colored Cadillac parked two blocks away from the docks. Inside, she pulled off her bow and laid it on the floor of the car. She then pulled off her bandolier and arrow sheath. Finally, she pulled off her form-fitting mask and shook her head. As she did a form appeared next to the driver's door. Ronald opened the door and slid behind the wheel. The Shrike sighed to herself and spoke, "I was just getting worried Ronald."

As he started the car he answered, "Sorry, ma'am. I had to knock down a police officer and hide under the pier for a while."

The Shrike undid her pony tail and shook her hair loose. She then carefully pulled off her boot to examine her heel, "It's all right. I'm just glad we both made it out safely."

Ronald laughed as he pulled the big car out into the street, "The rest of them weren't so lucky. I think the police got most of them."

"Good. That will put a crimp in our smuggler's Philadelphia plans."

"Yes, ma'am. I'm just sorry we couldn't net him as well."

"You did fine. We have people using your information now."

"Where to now, ma'am?"

"North. We have business in New York." Ronald nodded and the Cadillac purred away into the night.

• • •

Four days later Dixie handed a completed article to her editor and walked back to her desk. It was a report about visiting European royalty. It hadn't been hard to write up. She had managed it handily while digging out the latest information the Shrike had requested. Shaking her head she gathered up her purse and coat. Adjusting her hat at a jaunty angle she made for the elevator. Once on the street she fought the rush hour crowd uptown to the nearest subway entrance. On the platform she waited amongst the crowd for the next train.

Soon she became aware of a figure that had crowded in next to her. It was a short, petite woman dressed conservatively and carrying a large purse. Dixie attempted to get a look at the woman's face as she slipped the envelope she was carrying from her purse and into the woman's purse but was frustrated by the large hat she was wearing. As she did Dixie murmured, "Someone took a lot of trouble to cover their tracks but I found out all I could. It's all in there." The petite woman nodded without replying and stepped forward as a train roared into the station preceded by a wave of air pushed from the tunnel. Dixie held her ground and watched the woman disappear into the crowded car. The doors closed and Dixie turned away as the train sped into another dark tunnel.

• • •

That night the Shrike slipped down the alley behind a brownstone near Greenwich Village. She unlocked the back door and slipped inside. Once behind the locked door she moved through a darkened kitchen. In the hall she hung her dark cloak on a hook and climbed the stairs. She entered a room and turned on the light. There she unstrung her bow and hung it on the wall near several others. She removed her bandolier and arrow sheath and laid them on a crowded work bench. She left there and entered a simply furnished bedroom where she changed out of her gray outfit into a simple blouse and skirt. Once changed, she climbed to the third floor and entered a large room overlooking the street. She moved across the room and turned on a goose neck lamp that illuminated the top of a large desk. On the desk was an envelope marked *Report from Dickson.*

Sitting down behind the desk the Shrike tore open the envelope and began going over the contents carefully. As usual Dixie's research was clear and meticulous. She had been tasked with tracking down the new owners of the *Southern Star* shipping line. Dixie's research showed the company had recently been bought by a firm in Virginia after a series of accidents had driven the company near to bankruptcy. The Virginia firm was newly registered and apparently owned nothing but *Southern Star.* The Virginia firm was in turn registered to an individual living in Connecticut. Dixie had tracked this man down and found that he did not exist. Phony address, no birth certificate or any other record of him existed. Frustrated she had finally spent an entire day calling commercial real estate brokers until she finally found someone who remembered that name. Her report ended with an address in midtown.

Meanwhile the Shrike had spent the last few days around the docks. She had observed and followed several suspects. She had rousted a couple of them but they seemed to know very little. They were paid to turn a blind eye to an activity or carry something on or off a ship. She hadn't expected much. Now she had the information she had been waiting for. Tomorrow she would have a new target to watch.

The next night the hall door of a darkened office opened. A figure slipped inside and closed the door. A flashlight beam then cut through the darkness. The small office was empty. There was not a single item of furniture in it. The Shrike could see that dust was thick on the floor everywhere but the area around the door where she was standing. There the dust had been disturbed by footprints. An envelope lay on the floor near the door, obviously slipped through the mail slot. Bending down the Shrike saw that the address matched the name on the frosted glass in the hall door. It was a meaningless name she had never heard of. The office was a mail drop only. The Shrike wasted no more time but slipped out quietly just as she had come.

A few evenings later a young man in a suit entered the same office building and took the elevator to the fourth floor. He walked boldly up to the same door that the Shrike had entered recently. He unlocked the door and entered. Not bothering to turn on the light he scooped up the two letters on the floor and placed them in his pocket. Re-locking the door he turned and walked to the elevator. Pressing the button to summon it he ignored the older woman carrying a mop and bucket just entering the stairwell.

On the street he strolled casually up the street two blocks to a subway entrance. Apparently in no hurry he waited patiently for a train going to the Bronx. Several other people were waiting for the train. He paid them no attention. On the car he sat, picked up a discarded newspaper and read it as the train made its way out of Manhattan. He stayed on the train until it was nearly to Jackson Heights and then got off there. A middle-aged woman got off at the same stop.

On the street he walked half a block to a modest Ford sedan, got in and drove away. The woman following him made no attempt to follow. Instead she pulled out a small note pad and scribbled down the car's license number which she had quickly memorized.

Later at her Manhattan refuge the Shrike picked up a telephone and made a call. It was answered by a male voice, "Hello."

"Mr. Hale. You know who this is?"

Alert now, the voice replied, "Yes, I remember."

"I have a favor to ask."

"Ask away. I owe you more than I can repay."

"I need to find out who this vehicle is registered to." She read off the number she had scribbled down.

"Yes, I can do that tomorrow."

"Fine. Call this number," she read it to him. "Thank you Mr. Hale."

"Any time." Both hung up almost simultaneously.

Two days later the same average looking young man, now carrying a briefcase and newspaper, took a subway into Manhattan from Queens. On the crowded train he was just one of thousands commuting to work in the city. He got off in mid-town and walked three blocks to a large, busy office building. People were streaming into the building and he found himself crowded into an elevator with several young women; secretaries going to their jobs in the many businesses in the building. Once out of the elevator he entered a busy office on the seventh floor. Behind him a young sandy-haired woman in conservative dress passed the office, lingering for a moment to take in the name painted on the door. She nodded thoughtfully and then took the next elevator down to the street.

Once there she hailed a taxi and one quickly swerved over to the curb for the attractive young girl. Inside she gave an address in Greenwich Village and leaned back. Arriving at her address the Shrike paid her cab and climbed several steps to the front door. She let herself in with a key and went to her third floor study. She sat at her desk and leaned back in her chair closing her eyes as she thought for a few minutes. She then sat up and began organizing the various papers on her desk. She added a handwritten note and stuffed everything into an envelope and addressed it to Delores Dickson care of the *New York Bulletin*. She then grabbed her hat and purse and walked several blocks to a post office where she mailed the envelope then walked back to her brownstone to prepare for the evening's work.

That evening the Shrike sat in her coupe on a darkened road on Long Island. The lights of a large house could be seen through the trees of a landscaped estate. She got out of her car, reached in and grabbed her bow. She checked her pistol, arrows and bandolier before setting off through the trees. Once where she could get a clear view of the mansion she stopped under the limbs of a large oak tree and peered around the trunk. The mansion was well lit. Lights were on all over the three-story house. A large car sat in a circular driveway at the front door under a portico. Not liking what she saw the Shrike decided to move around to the back of the house hoping for more shadows to assist her entry into the house.

As she started to move the front door opened. A man in a suit left the house and entered the car. In the bright lights under the portico the Shrike recognized the new owner of the mansion. As the car started the Shrike turned and ran for her coupe. Once there she tossed her bow in ahead of her and threw herself behind the wheel. She accelerated hard. Driving without lights was dangerous but soon enough she caught up with the sedan and slowed using its distant headlights to navigate.

They soon reached busier roads and the Shrike was able to turn on her headlights. She hung back trying not to be noticed and followed her man as he headed toward Manhattan. They were in Nassau County and had at least twenty miles so she settled in for the trip.

She followed the car through Queens, across the Brooklyn Bridge and south toward the lower east side. She almost lost him once at a red light but some aggressive driving soon put her close enough to see her quarry pull over to a curb and get out. The Shrike turned off her lights and coasted to a stop down the block. She watched the man disappear into a large dark space between two buildings. Looking around she realized they were in walking distance of some of the east side docks.

Grabbing up her bow the Shrike followed carefully down the darkened street. It was an older neighborhood undergoing renovation. Two older condemned masonry buildings flanked an open space where a modern skyscraper was being constructed. The tall metal skeleton could be seen silhouetted against the sky. The poor lighting on the street illuminated a high wooden fence that kept passersby from trespassing on the site. There was a closed wooden door in the fence. Ignoring it the Shrike jumped up and grabbed the top of the fence and levered herself upwards. Once above the level of the fence she could see that the entire construction site was dark except for small wooden shack near the fence. There a light was burning in an un-curtained window. She could see two men talking in the shack that was no doubt the office of the construction foreman. The rest of the surrounding area was in deep shadow.

The Shrike dropped to the ground on the darkened side of the fence and waited. When her eyesight had adjusted enough for her to make out potential obstacles on the ground she crept forward. Soon she was close enough to hear the men's conversation.

A well-educated voice was saying, "That ought to be enough to keep your people happy for now. With the disruptions in Boston and Philadelphia it may take time to raise more cash."

Another voice answered, "Yeah, this'll grease some palms...Say, the word on the docks is the Feds raided some places down in Philly. Was that...?"

"...Not your concern!" the first voice answered sharply. "Your job is to keep things moving. You are ready for the *Castletown* arriving tomorrow night?"

"Yeah, I got the guys lined up...what was that?"

The Shrike had heard it also and quickly faded around the corner of the construction shack. It was the screech of rusty hinges as the door in the wooden fence opened. She crept behind it as she heard the shack's door open and the two men inside stepped out to meet the newcomer. Once on the other side she moved to a corner where she could see him.

He was bundled in a top coat and hat obviously trying to remain as anonymous as possible. The young man who the Shrike had followed from Long Island stepped forward, "Ah Hart. Glad you could make it."

The new man was clearly startled by the use of his name. He visibly started when saw the third somewhat roughly dressed man, "Who's he?"

"This is another of my... associates. Here for the same reason you are." He held out something to the new man who took it and examined it as best as could in the dim light, "I can't see. Is it all there?"

"Everything we agreed upon. As long as you hold up your end there will be additional, regular payments."

"The man nodded as he stowed the packet away in his over coat pocket. The Shrike wasn't sure exactly who this newcomer was but she had heard enough. She now had the man she wanted red handed. She nocked an arrow and stepped forward, "Everyone stand very still!"

She was only visible as a vague shadow in the semi-darkness but every one turned toward sound of her voice. "That's right Weatherby, I mean you." The man in the suit visibly started and stepped back against the wall of the shack, "How did—?"

Simultaneously the man in the topcoat said, "Who's he?"

Ignoring the other two men the Shrike kept her bow trained on the man in the suit, "How did I know who you are Weatherby? I know everything about you and your operation. And I'm here to put an end to it and put you behind bars."

Weatherby tried to stall, "I don't know who you are but you've made a mistake. I'm just here to meet—"

"It doesn't matter who you were here to pay off. They're going to jail too—"

Concentrating on Weatherby the Shrike didn't see the roughly dressed man's hand creeping toward his waistband in the darkness. She was surprised when he came up with a revolver in his hand but not so surprised that she couldn't pivot slightly and loose an arrow that went straight into his throat. The man crumpled to the ground with a gurgle, his gun firing into the ground. Using this slight diversion Weatherby reached for a gun of his own. He was bringing it up when the Shrike's second arrow went through his arm pinning it and him to the wall of the construction shack. Weatherby screamed in pain, dropped his gun and grabbed helplessly at his pinned arm.

As the Shrike pivoted toward the third man, reaching for an arrow as she turned, he yelled out, "Don't move!"

He also had drawn a revolver and had the Shrike covered. She stood motionless. He raised the gun toward her and yelled, "Drop the bow!"

The Shrike hesitated just a moment then dropped her bow into the shadows at her feet. The man in the overcoat seemed to relax a little so the Shrike let her hands drop. Just as with the big man she was mostly in shadow and her last opponent didn't see the pistol at her waist.

She brought it up firing low. He got off one shot that breezed past the Shrike's head. Her shots were better aimed and the man went down screaming as he grabbed for his leg. The Shrike looked around. The construction site was silent save for the moaning of the two wounded men. She walked past the pathetic figure of Weatherby into the shack. As she expected there was a telephone. She picked it up, lifted the receiver to her ear and asked the operator for the police.

Two minutes later she stepped out of the shack and over to Weatherby who was supporting his pinned arm and sobbing. She spoke quietly, "It's all over now Weatherby. The police are on the way. You're going to answer for the murder of your father, the kidnapping of Amy Farley and more crimes than I have time to count now.

"It wasn't enough that you were going to inherit your father's business someday. Instead you used your contacts to set up smuggling rings. But that wasn't enough either so you decided to use your father's business to enlarge your smuggling empire. Somehow your father got wind of what you were up to so he had to be eliminated. That gave you control of his shipping line as well as the power and contacts to really grow your operation. Unfortunately that murder was the beginning of the end for you. Now you're going to pay for everything you've done."

It couldn't be seen in the darkness but Weatherby's face had gone deathly pale...and not from blood loss, "But...but how could you—"

The Shrike didn't bother replying; instead she pulled out a handkerchief and held it out to him, "Press that to your wound. I wouldn't want you to bleed to death before the police get here. She turned away.

Over her shoulder she heard Weatherby gasp out, "Who *are* you?"

She moved to the man on the ground. He was moaning and holding his wounded leg. She pulled his belt loose and wrapped it around the leg to slow the bleeding. As she did she said to him, "Who are you?"

His eyes fixed on her frightening mask he whispered, "My name is Hart."

The Shrike pulled a stack of banded cash from his overcoat and waved it under his nose, "And why are you taking a payoff from Weatherby?"

"Uh I, uh—"

She yanked on the makeshift tourniquet making the man gasp. She could barely make out his pale and sweating face in the dim light. He swallowed and whispered, "Customs. I'm a customs inspector."

The Shrike stuffed the money back into the man's coat pocket. Standing up she looked down on him, "I would imagine you'll get the cell next to Weatherby. You can discuss your next project together for the next few years." Picking up her bow she turned and walked to her car.

The sounds of sirens came to her as she reached the coupe. She started it and drifted along the street slowly without lights. She pulled over near the corner and ducked down just a police car roared around the corner, siren blaring. It screeched to a stop in front of the construction site and two police men jumped out. Other sirens could be heard approaching. The Shrike nodded. She pulled off her hood, sat up and drove quietly away as the two policemen entered the construction site with flashlights.

• • •

Two days later Dixie sat at her desk holding up a copy that morning's paper. The headline read: *Smuggling Ring Smashed* in large print. The byline was smaller but clearly read Delores Dickson. She smiled. If she wasn't wearing a skirt and she smoked she would have put her feet up on the desk and lit up one of Fred's cigars. She had been accepting congratulations, some rather grudgingly, from other reporters all morning and it felt good. Now *this* was journalism.

She was snapped back to reality by Fred Sims appearing at her elbow, "That was good work, Dixie. A fine piece of writing." She looked up somewhat surprised, "Why thanks, Fred. That's good to hear."

He nodded, "I hope you do half as well on this." He handed her a slip of paper. As he turned away he said, "The mayor's holding a luncheon to help raise money for some new civic improvement plan or something. Go cover it."

Dixie opened her mouth to protest but instead sighed, bent forward and gently rested forehead against the blotter. She sighed, "You can't win for losing around here."

• • •

It was growing dark in the valley. To the west the last glow of the setting sun could be seen over the hills. Shadows were deep along the road that cut through the valley and among the trees on the wooded slopes. Staring out through the picture window the Shrike could see the first lights appearing from the scattering of homes on the other side of the valley. She turned as steps approached.

A petite, young blonde woman handed her a snifter of amber colored liquid and smiled. The Shrike brushed back a strand of her light brown hair and accepted the glass, "Thank you Karen."

Karen walked across the large, comfortably furnished room to a long sofa and sat at one end. She slipped off her shoes and curled her legs under her as she sipped her own drink, "What are you thinking so hard about?"

The Shrike sipped and turned once more to the darkening scene outside the window, "I'm just considering things."

"Well, it seems like everything came out well. Weatherby is in jail, as are most of his people. With all the evidence that you gave Miss Dickson and sent to the police they'll be arresting people for weeks. And best of all, you saved that little girl." She sipped from her glass and added, "Not to mention none of us got killed. It seems like a happy ending to me. By the way, how's your foot?"

"Healing. It was just a scrape anyway, although I'm going to need a new pair of boots."

"A small price to pay."

The Shrike sipped and added, "How's the repair work on the coupe coming?"

"Ronald says it's just a couple of bullet holes. Nothing penetrated the armor."

The Shrike ran her hand through her long hair and looked pre-occupied. Karen frowned and asked, "What's bothering you?"

"What do you think of Dickson?"

"Well, she may be a bit headstrong but it seems she was helpful. Did she get rattled when the bullets were flying?"

The Shrike frowned, "No, she did fine there. She kept her head when things got tough but—"

"—you worry about her," Karen finished.

Yes, she's a wild card. She overstepped her orders and things could have gone very wrong for her and the Farley girl."

"So we keep an eye on her. She's too good an asset to lose."

"I agree. She is valuable but we will need to keep her on a short rope. She tends to be too enthusiastic."

Karen nodded, and then added, "Oh, I almost forgot. A package came for you today. I put it on your work bench. It's got a Florida postmark—"

"Good. Sam claims to have been working on something new."

Karen smiled slyly, "It *was* kind of heavy for its size."

The Shrike moved over to the fireplace and held out a hand to the crackling flames. Karen sipped and queried from the sofa, "So what's next?"

The Shrike turned and a sharpness came into her eyes, "I have word there's something going on out west. We may be making a trip to Chicago soon."

Karen smiled, "If we're traveling I'm going to have to do some shopping." Both women laughed out loud together.

• • •

In a building in the heart of Washington D.C., a man sat at desk in an office with the door closed. He was a tall man of middle age, with an intelligent face and a hard look about his eyes. He was in shirt sleeves, his suit jacket hanging on the coat tree next to his hat. A badge was on his belt to the right of his buckle and a revolver hung under his left arm. The name plate on his desk read *Wallendor*. He stubbed out a cigarette in an ash tray and picked up the letter again. It had come in the mail that day from Philadelphia along with a package. He re-read the salient passage:

> *So in response to your memo, I am forwarding the accompanying item recovered at a warehouse in this city on the 9th of this month at the scene of a major smuggling arrest by federal agents. It has been logged in as evidence but we do not need it as we have others, or at least the remains of others. I hope this is the kind of thing you are looking for. If you get the chance, I (and a few others) would like to know why you are looking for this kind of evidence. Everyone at this field office thinks it was pretty strange. If I can be of further service please feel free to contact me.*
>
> *Sincerely,*
>
> *Charlie Banks*
> *Special Agent, FBI*

The tall man set down the letter and picked up an object from his desk. It was a metal shaft a little over a quarter inch in diameter and almost a foot long, apparently made of aluminum. The interesting thing about it was the feathers set in three equally spaced rows around the diameter at one end. The other end was rough and appeared to be melted by some extreme heat. He set the shaft down and went to a nearby filing cabinet. He unlocked it and searched through some files folders. Finding the one the he wanted he pulled the thick folder out and returned to his desk.

Sitting down he lit up another cigarette and opened the file marked **Shrike?** in bold letters. As he did he decided to give agent Banks a call. He must have an interesting story to tell.

THE END

BIRTH OF THE SHRIKE

The Shrike; hmmm...well I didn't actually set out to create the *Shrike*... she actually came as somewhat of a surprise to me. It started this way: Last year I wrote a story for *Airship 27s* new *Domino Lady* anthology. I was excited about the story but also a little wary. I had never written a female hero before especially one who was a lot different from the characters I had been writing about. So with some trepidation I went ahead on the project and...I had a ball. I enjoyed the story so much a few months later I wrote another *Domino Lady* story that should appear in the second Airship 27 anthology.

Having discovered how much fun female heroes could be, I cast around for another character to write about. I decided a female crime reporter operating out of New York might be fun, so I worked up a profile and pitched it to Ron Fortier at Airship 27. Initially Ron was cool to the idea. He said the idea had been done before. He then told me he did want new female characters but what he would like to see done was a female pulp avenger character.

I mulled this over, looked through some old notes and wrote Ron asking what exactly he had in mind. He replied that he thought a Shadow-like character would work well. A character that was wealthy, with lots of esoteric skills who had traveled the world and had a network of operatives to help her in her crusade against crime.

Now The Shadow has always been my favorite pulp character. I have read dozens of Shadow adventures and still find them quite readable. I especially enjoyed the early stories in the series. In those his operatives often did a lot of the investigative work with the Shadow hovering in the background waiting to swoop in at the critical moments. Those early stories had a certain air of mystery because we didn't see or know too much about the Shadow. He was a true man of mystery. This was just the kind of thing I was looking for. So I pulled a few Shadow novels out of my library and skimmed through them for inspiration. I then went back to my roleplaying days and resurrected a character I had created and, voila', the Shrike was born.

Back in my roleplaying days I had a character that was a cross between Marvel's Hawkeye and Moon Man. He had a background and skill set that would fit perfectly for my female avenger character. I changed a few things, added some skills and came up with a great basis for the Shrike. As for operatives; there are unlimited possibilities there and I have some interesting ones in my bag of tricks, a few I used in this story. You may have noticed the Shrike's operative, Dixie? Yes, she is the reporter character I initially pitched to Ron. She worked out extremely well as one of the Shrike's operatives and hopefully we will see more of her in the future; perhaps in her own adventure. I think she is too good a character to disappear totally. After all who doesn't like a nosy, but attractive and engaging female reporter?

What about he Shrike's history I hear someone asking. Who is she? What's her background? Why was there no origin story? Well, taking another leaf from Walter Gibson's playbook, the Shrike will remain mysterious for a while. There are a few clues in this story to her background but plenty of questions as well. This was intended. I plan on writing more Shrike stories; perhaps lots of them. They will run the length and breadth of her career and clues as to her origin will be scattered throughout them.

So that's how the Shrike came about. She is certainly my creation but Ron Fortier deserves credit for inspiring me to write the story as well as his valuable input in how I wrote her. I am thankful for his input and pleased that she is coming to life in an Airship 27 publication.

So will we see her again soon? Perhaps. If you liked The Shrike let Ron know. I have more of her adventures outlined and would jump at the chance to write more of them. Thanks for reading and making The Shrike's debut a success. See you for her next adventure.

• • •

GENE MOYERS - studied European and Medieval history at the University of Oregon. He is also a U.S. Army veteran. He worked in the high tech industry for some time and ran a store front and internet hobby shop for several years.

An avid military gamer and role player, his favorite game was *Daredevils* a pulp based roleplaying game set in the 1930s. His love affair with the 1930s and pulps in particular stem from his first time reading a *Shadow* novel as a boy. Although interested in writing since a teen he did not turn to serious writing until 2000. He is the co-author of *GURPS Crusades* published by Steve Jackson Games. He has now written several stories for Airship 27 including stories featuring *Ravenwood, The Purple Scar, The Moon Man, The Domino Lady and The Phantom Detective*. He has also written adventure stories for Pro Se Press anthologies.

When not working on various new pulp projects he is busy writing horror adventures for his swashbuckling character set in Colonial America. Gene currently lives in Beaverton, Oregon with his wife and three lazy dogs.

LOST IN THE FLOOD
(A NIGHTBREAKER ADVENTURE)

By Thomas Deja

Benjamin Cameron sat at the old desk in his study. On his blotter were scattered a number of reports. His eyes were heavy from lack of sleep. The only source of light was an overhead lamp that bathed the papers in a soft, yellowish luminescence. A full moon could be seen between the slightly parted white linen curtains.

His family slept in the bedrooms below. Benjamin knew that this was his inherent weakness—he couldn't keep his mind off his work for too long. He worried that his two children would grow up with only a dim memory of their father; that they might end up resenting him as adults. But there were people here in Nocturne who counted on him to safeguard their money, and he took that responsibility seriously.

He glanced at the clock quickly. It was moving slowly towards midnight. He began to feel heaviness in his limbs.

"Maybe it is time for bed," he muttered to himself before standing up and stepping away from the desk. He yawned as he gathered up the reports and returned them to the file cabinet. Once everything was back in its place, he headed for the door, but stopped well before his goal.

The carpet, it seemed, was wet.

Benjamin looked down upon the spot where the fibers were moist. The house was old, and sometimes the roof leaked. But the staff always managed to patch the damage before it got out of hand. His attention went to the roof, eyes squinting to see if he could find the spot where the water is coming from.

And the roof creaked.

Not the creaking of a house settling. The creaking of something beginning to fall apart.

Benjamin ran to the door as the creak became a rumble of masonry falling apart. Pieces of stone suddenly fell to the floor, accompanied by a powerful deluge. He turned the knob with the intention of fleeing, but he never left the room...for the inrush of water actually changed direction, enveloping him in a bubble of liquid.

And as Benjamin Cameron breathed his last, outside the warm, dry summer night bore witness.

• • •

Isaiah Copper laid back in his chaise lounge and let the sun wash over his face. His wife sat to his left in a similar lounge, and a pitcher of lemonade lay between them. The air was thick with the sounds of birds and insects. He grasped his half full glass, dotted with condensation and allowed himself a smile.

"What?" Gloria Copper asked. Months of training with Isaiah's ally in the Shadow Legion Maybelle Tremens allowed his wife to see him even when he was out of phase with reality.

"It's nothing."

"Well it must be something to have you grinning like an old Jack O'Lantern."

He craned his neck to look at his wife. Once again, he wondered why he had the luck to marry the most beautiful woman in this city. "Just thinking how perfect today is."

She playfully swatted him on the arm. "Go on now!"

"No, it's true." Isaiah sat up and looked his wife in the eye. "You weren't with me those weeks I was ignored by everyone. I despaired of ever having an afternoon like this one, sitting next to you and enjoying the day, again."

Gloria made a face. "Well, I don't believe you, but thank you for the compliment."

"You're always welcome, love."

The phone rang from inside the house. Gloria made a sour face and got up from her seat. Isaiah sipped his lemonade and watched her. "Damnable people have to interrupt us all the time. I've got a hankering to give them a piece of my mind."

"Don't be so harsh on them. They don't know what we're doing."

Isaiah took a deep breath of contentment as his wife went into the house and answered the phone. Given his choice, he would live like this forever. Maybelle had warned him that Midnight Men like himself tended to live way beyond a normal lifespan, and that he may see his wife wither with age while he remained the same. Knowing that, he would try his best to enjoy as much of a life with Gloria as he could.

He was aware of the faint conversation Gloria was having with the phone caller. It sounded as if his wife was annoyed with the person on the other end of the line.

Before he could settle in more, Gloria opened the back window and called out, "Honey, it's for you. It's that Munchen fella!"

Isaiah sighed. He knew his moment of contentment was going to be short-lived.

• • •

Isaiah pulled up to the old Tudor mansion in Farshore. He was dressed as the avenger known as Nightbreaker. Once, long ago, Isaiah was just a radio actor portraying the character. But then a moment of heroism threw him out of dimensional phase. Now unable to be perceived by others unless he concentrate on a mental mantra—a being an ally of his referred to as a Midnight Man—he took on the identity of Nightbreaker as a way to be acknowledged, to be told that he existed.

The tall, lanky form of Detective Munchen waited for him at the front door, a cigarette dangling from his lips. "I saw this, and I knew it was right up your alley."

"You are too kind, Detective," Isaiah shot back as he made his way up the walk.

Munchen adjusted his glasses and opened the door. "You ready for this one?"

"As I'll ever be."

The detective led Isaiah through the foyer into the main room. Towards the center, Isaiah felt a coldness in the soles of his feet. He looked down to see the carpet was sodden with water. His eyes went upwards, and there was a large dark stain on the ceiling.

"What the...?"

Munchen took to the stairs. "You'll find out once we get upstairs."

Nightbreaker followed his friend. The whole house spoke of old money. It made him feel self-conscious even with all the times he visited his allies at Palmersdale House.

The trail led from the stairs down a corridor to a wooden door towards the back of the house. Even from this side of the door, Nightbreaker could see something was wrong. There was a dark patch seeping under the threshold. The stain wasn't tinged with red, which made his curiosity rise. He watched as Munchen slipped on some latex gloves and pushed open the door for him.

The room was dripping with water. It soaked the carpet thoroughly, turned the library into so much sodden pulp and practically warped some of the furniture. It was as if the entire space had been filled from top to bottom with liquid and allowed to drain naturally. Scattered across the floor were jagged pieces of wood and tile.

"No pipes, no water storage on the roof, and it was a bone dry night," Munchen said as he stepped into the room. His feet squelched with each step. "At least you're wearing boots; I've ruined these shoes."

Nightbreaker wandered into the area. The place was steamy, the results of so much water evaporating in the hot summer sun. Above them the roof was caved in, with a beam of sunlight cascading down to highlight the carnage.

"I see why you suspect involvement of specials like me."

Munchen pulled a book from the library; its cover was warped beyond much recognition. "Well, people like you are springing up with alarming rapidity, and it stands to reason that some of these new guys won't follow your example."

"Can I get onto the roof?"

"You have that grapple hook; you tell me."

Nightbreaker went out to the lawn—the very dry lawn—and aimed his grapple gun. In a second, the line was attached to the roof. He climbed up the wall, something he wished he didn't have as much experience at as he did.

The hole was just as bizarre as the crime scene. Water stains had circled it, but the rest of the roof seemed to be dry. He walked the length and breadth of the roof, looking for similar marks but came up with nothing.

It only emphasized the belief that a special, one who utilized water in some way, was responsible for the death of Benjamin Cameron.

And the only way to figure out anything about this special lay in figuring out Cameron.

• • •

Benjamin Cameron had a small office in Tyson Quad along with his partner Gerard Drake. This made his firm uniquely apart from all the other investment bankers who plied their trade along Bartholomew Avenue in Jubilee. When Nightbreaker and Detective Munchen arrived at the building, it was noon. The midday sun beat down on the duo, as it had for over a week.

They took the stairs up to the third floor of the building, an older edifice that dated back to the time of the reconstruction. Munchen knocked on the door—there was no bell—and waited for the brightly smiling receptionist to let them in.

The receptionist was a pretty blonde with a dimpled smile. She showed a bit of surprise upon seeing Nightbreaker in his full uniform, but didn't show it in her voice. "How may I help you?"

Munchen showed his badge. "We're here to see Mr. Drake."

She stepped aside to let them in. "This is about poor Mr. Cameron, isn't it? He was such a good man to work for. Have a seat and I'll get Mr. Drake."

Munchen settled himself down in a nearby wooden chair. Nightbreaker stood, choosing to study some of the portraits on either side of the room. It seemed that the firm of Cameron and Drake was a generational operation.

After a few minutes, a rotund man with a fringe of red hair came out. He extended a hand. "Gentlemen, I'm Gerard Drake."

Munchen shook the man's hand. "Thank you for seeing us."

"It's my...well, it's macabre to say it's a pleasure, given the circumstances. Please come in."

Nightbreaker followed the two into the man's office. It was a fair sized room with Drake's desk of oiled walnut before a window looking out on the skyline in the distance. Pictures placed along a small bar depicted the man posing with a deer he had just shot. A portrait of a man who resembled Drake was hung off to the side. Nightbreaker got the sense of old money from the place. Drake motioned towards a pair of chairs that looked older than all of them. "Please take a seat."

Nightbreaker and Munchen lowered themselves into their seats. As Drake sat down, he said, "It isn't everyday I play host to such an unusual celebrity."

"I wouldn't call myself a celebrity," Nightbreaker said.

"Nonsense. You're an icon in this city. You were one before you were, ah, real." Drake templed his fingers. "I understand this is about what happened to poor Benjamin."

"Yes," Munchen responded.

"I thought what happened to him was a freak accident."

"Given the presence in this town of humans with special powers," Nightbreaker said, "we're not ruling out that it was more sinister than that. Do you know of anyone who had a grudge against Mr. Cameron?"

Drake shrugged. "Personally? No. But we are in the business of managing other people's money, and sometimes customers don't like the way we do that managing."

"Anyone in particular stands out? Someone who may have threatened him?"

"Not that I recall. But then, we do see many clients, and some get lost in our memories."

"Of course," said Munchen. The detective took off his glasses and pinched the bridge of his nose. "Anyone with a technological background?"

"Sometimes these special people utilize mechanical means to give them their abilities," added Nightbreaker.

"Certainly we have tech clients. What with the Silver Spire boom, a lot of the technological firms have come to us to invest. I can look into my records to see if anything jumps out."

"We'd appreciate that."

"If you can forward what you find to me," Munchen said, handing Drake his card. "I would appreciate it."

The detective and Nightbreaker stood up. They made for the door. However, the hero stopped before leaving.

"Think about people who might have a grudge in his personal life as well," Nightbreaker said. "Anyone who might be disgruntled towards Mr. Cameron."

Drake seemed taken aback by the comment. "I don't know if I can help you as much there. Benjamin and I were friendly, but I wouldn't say we were friends."

"Still, whatever you come up with will be helpful."

As they left, Munchen said, "What was that all about?"

"Just a hunch," Nightbreaker replied. "Revenge is not usually the first thought of someone who had financial disagreements. It's much more a personal thing."

• • •

Nightbreaker surveyed what passed for the Lincoln skyline. While large areas of Nocturne were building upwards, creating a new look for *The City That Lives By Night*, his old neighborhood still appeared broken down and old, buildings rarely more than two stories. The only exception these days was off to the hero's right, a new office block that his friend Colin Palmersdale had commissioned, a modern edifice that would rise above the world's toughest area. It was almost finished, and according to Colin some firms had already signed on to become tenants. He hoped this was the first of many new construction projects that would raise Lincoln up by its bootstraps.

He pulled out his line thrower and cast it across the street. The crampon affixed itself to a cornice of a decaying brick building. Nightbreaker swung out, taking some pleasure in the feel of the wind across his body. He moved over the street and released the strong nylon line to land on the opposite roof. Tar paper was peeling from the concrete surface in reaction to the muggy night. He moved across the rooftops speedily, his eyes and ears open for something that required his attention.

Nightbreaker felt more comfortable here, dealing with the street crime of his old neighborhood. Yes, he was always there when his Shadow Legion allies needed him for their supernatural conflict. Yes, he had some macabre experiences himself. But he always felt out of depth even with his own peculiar power and his versatile weapon, the Multi-Gun. He belonged here, sweeping up the human detritus who were insistent on dragging the neighborhood down.

A scream rent the night. Nightbreaker looked toward the source of the disturbance and took off at a run.

He found his way to an alley that stank of urine and garbage. A woman was pushed up against the wall by a hulking brute of a man. Her hat was on the ground, and her clothes were disheveled. The man's knife glinted in the moonlight. Nightbreaker unholstered the Multi-Gun and aimed it at the man. "Get away from her!"

The man's head swiveled on its bull neck. He smiled, displaying a row of rotting teeth, the gums receding. "You should get away from me, masked man," he said, dropping his victim.

"Don't say I didn't warn you," Nightbreaker responded. He thumbed the cylinders of his Multi-Gun and fired. The man was thrown back into the back of the alley by the impact payload. Nightbreaker closed the distance between himself and the woman's attacker. He straddled the man and punched him hard in the face. The man snarled and brought his foot up into Nightbreaker's crotch. The hero stumbled backwards a few steps, allowing his opponent to scramble for his knife. Nightbreaker raised his Multi-gun, his thumb already dialing up the proper payload and fired not at the man but his weapon just as he reached it. Electricity arced from the payload to the knife to the man's hand. The brute suddenly pulled away his arm, his fingers singed. As his enemy struggled to his feet, Nightbreaker launched a massive roundhouse, utilizing his weapon as a club. Blood and teeth flew as the man's head snapped back. Nightbreaker continued his offensive, moving closer and planting a fist into the man's solar plexus. Air went out of his enemy, and he doubled over. Nightbreaker drove a knee into the man's chin. The man stumbled, swayed and finally fell to the ground insensate.

Nightbreaker aimed his Multi-Gun at the unconscious assailant. It barked once, producing a payload that tied him up in tough filaments. He holstered his weapon and approached the woman. Her wide eyes were made even wider by fear. Tears streaked her mascara. "You're safe now."

"I g-gave him my purse," she stammered out, "but...he wanted more."

"Well, he's in no condition to hurt you now. Do you have a dime?"

The woman nodded.

"Go call the police. Even if he wakes up, he won't be in any condition to come after you."

The woman scrabbled against the wall until she was on her feet. She took off, first at a walk, but increasing speed with each step.

Nightbreaker looked down at the attacker. If things had been different, if he had taken another path, if Lincoln was the kind of neighborhood that nurtured its young...

All wishes that never went anywhere. Looking at the past of Lincoln wasn't going to help the future.

Nightbreaker unclipped his line thrower. He turned, prepared to leave, when in the distance the sound of rushing water drew his attention. He re-aimed his line thrower in the direction of the noise and fired.

It could be nothing, he realized. But after seeing what happened in Cameron's house, he had to investigate. The Nocturne air was hot and humid. The skies were clear.

As he swung out over Page Street, he could see where the noise had come from. There was in front of him a three-story tenement, its crumbling concrete facade making it look barely habitable for human beings. On the third floor, water trailed from the windows. It etched trails in the filth covering the building, pooling on the street.

Without hesitation, Nightbreaker swung onto the building's roof. There was a pool of liquid in the middle of the tarry surface. He waded through the extended puddle, his boots discoloring from the contact with the water. The roof access door was open. He slipped inside and went down the stairs, heading for the floor directly underneath.

There were two apartments on the floor, one in the front and one in the back. The door of the back apartment was open a crack, and Nightbreaker could see someone hiding behind it, keeping an eye on what was going on. "Call the police," he said and headed toward the front apartment.

His boots squished on the welcome mat. He reached into a compartment on his belt and produced a set on lockpicks. A few seconds worth of effort opened the door.

Inside, the fixtures were dripping with water. The overhead light bulbs had the darkened area that indicated that they had burned out. There were puddles of water everywhere. Dark stains rimmed the bottom of the furniture.

He found the body at the threshold of the den. A black woman with her hair tied up in a kerchief, her generous figure bloated from the liquid she had apparently had forced down her throat. Her limbs were at odd angles, like a marionette with her strings cut. Nightbreaker knelt down next to the corpse and looked for some indication of who she was. There was nothing in her nightdress.

On one of the cabinets he found a wallet. The driver's license within had identified her as Rachel Jericho. There were a few sodden dollar bills folded inside, but other than that, nothing.

Nightbreaker left the apartment looking for a pay phone. It was time to call Dectective Munchen.

• • •

The Detective looked down at the dead woman's face just before she was zipped into a body bag. Other police personnel were scouring the apartment for clues and evidence.

Munchen scratched the back of his head. "She looks familiar."

"How so?" Nightbreaker asked.

"I'm not sure." the detective responded.

Nightbreaker watched the coroner's assistants carry out the body. "All I know is we have two dead people now and they have no connection."

"When it comes to murders this similar, there's always a connection."

"What about Jack The Ripper?"

Munchen looked at him sideways. "There was a connection. It's just that no one's ever figured it out."

Nightbreaker checked his Multi-Gun. There was need for some different payloads. "I'll take to the streets; see if anyone knows anything about our serial drowner."

"Do that. I'll use more conventional methods. I just hope we can find that connection before this perp strikes again."

"We'll catch him," Nightbreaker said quietly. "You know we will."

• • •

It was early in the morning when Nightbreaker returned to the seemingly abandoned gas station that was his secret sanctum. He descended into his workshop and removed his bandana and goggles, placing them on a steel table near the entrance.

His mind was contemplating this unusual foe. Apparently this person had some control over water. He or she had used it in both of the murders, and the fact that portions of Cameron's roof was bone dry indicated there was a level of control. There had to be a key to shutting this being down.

Of course, a more nagging question was how this being was choosing his victims. His detective friend's comment about there having to be a connection stuck with them. The more he thought about it, Nightbreaker realized, the more he began to suspect there was something to it.

He went to a table with a pile of payload shells atop it. It was only a matter of time, he knew, when he would have to face off against this water-using personage. It would make sense to prepare ahead of time. Nightbreaker wondered if he should call in his friend Jenny Argo to pick her brain.

He began to gather up tools and equipment. This was going to take a while.

• • •

Paulie Kennedy was not what you would call a mover and shaker, and that suited him just fine. He was much more comfortable on the fringes of the underworld, observing the various mayhem from a safe distance. And if someone wanted the information he gathered, and if that someone had some money, all the better.

He gathered his threadbare woolen coat about him as he walked down the street. His rheumy brown eyes scanned from left to right and back again. His mind was on the one room apartment he lived in, and the oscillating fan he planned on sitting in front of to cool himself off. This day did not produce much in the way of information he could sell; it was all petty stuff that would only net him a handful of change.

Paulie had turned the corner onto Bell Boulevard when the line had hooked onto his coat and pulled him up several stories. He screamed in surprise. The sidewalk receded until it was a narrow strip of concrete. Paulie suddenly worried that he would not survive the drop.

Looking up, he saw a masked figure extending his hand. "Better take it, Paulie. Don't know how much longer I can hold you up."

Paulie grabbed hold of the offered gloved hand. He was pulled up onto the roof. Paulie lay there looking up at the sky. His breathing slowed. "What are you trying to do, scare me half to death? 'Cause you did," he complained.

"I could have made it worse," Nightbreaker responded, putting away his line thrower. "You're just lucky I have a soft heart."

He began to gather up tools and equipment. This was going to take a while.

Paulie sat up. "What do you want?"

"What do I always want from you?"

"You're gonna have to be more specific." Paulie got to his feet and dusted himself off.

Nightbreaker walked towards Paulie. The snitch was once more made aware of how much larger the hero was. "There's a new player in town. Likes to drown people in the middle of dry land. Wondered if you heard anything."

"What, another super? You know me, 'breaker. I don't mess with people with powers like that. Too dangerous."

"And yet you sometimes find information about them," Nightbreaker said. His hand rested on his holstered Multi-Gun. "I need you to learn anything you can about our watergoing friend."

"That's going to cost you...expenses, hazard fees—"

"I suspect the NPD will make sure you're well compensated."

"See that I am."

Nightbreaker raised his line thrower and fired. The crampon buried itself into the rooftop across the street. "We'll be in touch," he told Paulie before swinging away.

• • •

"I knew there was a connection," Detective Munchen practically crowed. They were at Napoleon Circle late at night, the place where he and Nightbreaker usually met. Even at this advanced hour, there were still people wandering this central area of *The City That Lives By Night*. That these passers-by didn't react to a man dressed as a pulp hero standing before the statue of the Horae. The fact was most saw it as indicative of Nocturne's style.

"So Cameron and Jericho knew each other?"

Munchen opened up a manila folder. "They didn't *know* each other, but they did have a connection. I did a little digging on the woman...well, a lot of digging. I had to go into the county clerk's records before I hit paydirt."

Nightbreaker took the papers within the folder. He lifted the goggles onto his forehead to better read what was written there. He was silent as he took in the information.

"They were on a jury?" he asked Munchen.

"Along with ten other people," the detective replied. "All empaneled to determine the fate of one Scott Baker. This charmer tried to rob the Nocturne Federal Bank along with four others. Main difference is that Baker put a bullet through some teller's head."

"So he got a separate trial."

"Exactly. And it went as well as you would expect. Baker was sent off to Taylor for a good long time, only for him to be released recently on parole."

"Do we have a photo of this Mr. Baker?" Nightbreaker asked.

"Is there any doubt?" The Detective reached into another folder and handed the hero a photograph. It was a booking photo, and the subject had a gaunt face, sunken eyes and sparse hair. He smiled for the camera, a maddening enigmatic upturn of one side of his lips. There was a sense of disarray about the man, as if he had just gotten out of bed.

Nightbreaker handed back the photo. "Do we know where he is right now?"

Munchen shook his head. "Never reported in to his parole officer. His flophouse room was abandoned."

"So you think he's going back to settle the score on the jury that put him away?"

"It's my guess. I've already put in a requisition for men to help me cover the remaining jurors."

"Let me see the list."

Munchen handed Nightbreaker a piece of paper. The hero studied it for a minute. "The next name is Fredric Morai."

"Tailor. Has a shop in Tyson Quad, lives on the floor above. Two sons."

"You're doing your research."

"You think I sit around doing nothing at the precinct? This is my job."

"And you do it very well, Detective," Nightbreaker said. He handed the paper back to the tall gaunt man. "I think I'll keep an eye on this Mr. Morai tonight. Until you get your requisition approved—"

"*If* I get it approved," the detective responded.

"Regardless," the hero said, unclipping his line thrower. "We'll catch this Mr. Baker. I'll be in touch."

"Not if I get in touch with you first," Munchen said, watching his friend fire the line thrower and swing off.

• • •

The tailoring shop was wedged between two bars that offered live music. This was what you accepted in Tyson's Quad—given the plethora of entertainment spots, your business was more than likely going to be stuck next to one.

One if you were lucky.

Nightbreaker crouched across the street, goggles and kerchief around his neck, and kept watch over the tailor shop. Music wafted up from one of the venues on either side, what had recently begun to be called "rock n' roll." Nightbreaker was unsure of what to make of this new style of music after growing up with the great big bands of his era. The one thing it definitely did was remind him he was getting older, even if his body wasn't aging.

The shop on the first floor had been dark for an hour. He had watched Morai—a slight, small man with grey hair—close up before ascending to the second floor. Nightbreaker tried to imagine what he was doing now. It made him briefly melancholy, knowing his life would never be normal again. Ever since he slipped between this dimension and the next one in the ticks before midnight, his life was changed beyond restoring.

After the third hour, Nightbreaker was beginning to get restless. This was evidentially not going to be the night. The more active streets of Lincoln were tugging at his consciousness, and he was considering going there. He got up and stretched. The moon was shining down on him, painting him in shadows and silver.

And then something moved across the street.

It was hard to get a clear look at what rose from behind the tailor shop; its outline wavered randomly. It did have the vague outline of a man, although its lower half was one more or less smooth line. Nightbreaker pulled up his goggles and kerchief, once more disguising his face. He grabbed hold of his line thrower and fired.

It took a second to swing across to the roof of Morai's building. The bizarre figure had lit down upon the roof. It was a man in a tight blue hooded bodysuit. His face was hidden by a curious yellow mask that covered his nose and mouth. Tinted goggles concealed his eyes. His hands were bare, and yellow boots that had the same sheen as the mask were on his feet. But the thing that made the man so unusual was that he was enveloped in a man-shaped field of water.

"Mr. Baker, I assume," Nightbreaker said.

The man raised his head to acknowledge him. He was hovering over the ground, the water form connecting with the roof. Nightbreaker unlatched the holster of his Multi-Gun as the man in blue glided to him.

"I go by Flood now," the man said, his voice slightly distorted by the field of liquid. He flowed even closer. Nightbreaker was disturbed to see no air bubbles with the speech.

"Flood, then." Nightbreaker unholstered his signature weapon. In the back of his mind, he considered which payload to use. "You know I can't allow this journey of revenge to continue."

"I can't allow you to stop me."

"Then we'll have to disagree. You are going back to prison."

"I can't see how you can stop me," the man called Flood responded and raised his arm. He made a slashing movement, and suddenly a gout of water rocketed from his water form. Nightbreaker was hit with the force of a firehose. He fell to the roof and gripped the edge to prevent falling over.

Nightbreaker got to his knees. He raised the Multi-Gun, his thumb dialing in the electric payload. With the water surrounding him, Flood should be shocked into unconsciousness. His finger tightened on the trigger—

—and suddenly Flood motioned again, only this time the water reached out and engulfed Nightbreaker. Liquid surrounded him. He dropped the Multi-Gun and reached for his belt, his lungs already burning for air. Flood moved closer to him. "How does it feel, drowning on dry land?"

Nightbreaker pulled out a payload shell. He rapidly placed it over his mouth and flipped a switch on its side. He found himself able to breathe again as air was delivered to his mouth from inside the shell. Quickly, he dove to the left, out of the flow. Flood motioned with his hand and the stream of water followed him. Nightbreaker scrabbled away from the constant deluge, narrowly missing having the liquid engulf him again. He unclipped the line thrower and fired at his foe. The line entered the water field and slowed before it wrapped around Flood's ankle.

Nightbreaker got to his feet. Flood had retracted the water stream and stood defensively. The hero could see his weapon lying on the ground several feet away. He made a move towards the Multi-Gun, but Flood lashed out with a stream of water so powerful it knocked the curious looking gun over the edge of the roof.

"I'm going to do what I came to do," Flood promised.

Nightbreaker turned towards his watery foe and released the mantra that kept him anchored in this reality. To Flood, it looked as if Nightbreaker had vanished from view. But the hero just moved closer to the blue-garbed figure and leapt toward him, resuming the mantra as he left his feet. He hit Flood hard, holding him around the waist and launching the man out of his water envelope. Hero and villain hit the concrete roof hard. The mass of water suddenly collapsed, no longer having form. Flood gasped for air that was forced out of his lungs by the impact. Nightbreaker was on top of him and punched the man on the chin.

Flood managed to raise his arm. Before Nightbreaker could continue to pummel his foe, the water that soaked the roof rose up and slammed into him with the force of a speeding car. Nightbreaker fell off Flood, turning end over end until he hit the cornice of the chimney.

Stars exploded in Nightbreaker's vision. He stumbled forward, narrowly dodging another blast that chipped the brick surface. Flood was on his feet, gathering the water around him again. Nightbreaker rushed toward his foe and landed a blow to his chest. Another thrown punch was knocked away.

"You don't give up," Flood said.

"Never," Nightbreaker responded.

Flood punched Nightbreaker hard in the face, and again in the stomach. Nightbreaker's field of vision darkened. He swung wildly at the blue garbed man, but Flood easily dodged under it. The water pooling behind them had now once more become an envelope that surrounded Flood and lifted him up. He motioned once more, and a stream of water hit Nightbreaker in the chest. He was driven back to the roof. He found himself unable to keep his mantra going, so he slipped into his base dimension. On unsteady legs that felt like rubber, he tried to get to his feet only to fall again...

...and then everything went black.

• • •

He came to still in his dimension. Nightbreaker shook his head in an attempt to clear his befogged mind. He slowly got to his feet. Surrounding him, oblivious to his presence, were a pair of uniformed police officers and Detective Munchen. Nightbreaker headed for the chimney and propped himself up. He began to activate his mantra; to the trio it looked as if he appeared out of nowhere.

"There you are," drawled Munchen, putting his hands in his pocket.

"What did I miss?" Nightbreaker asked weakly.

"The man you've been guarding is dead for one thing. Drowned by Baker like the others."

"Flood."

Munchen scratched the back of his neck. "Pardon me?"

"He's picked out a villain name. Calls himself Flood."

"Well, we wouldn't have known that...we wouldn't have known this had happened if someone hadn't noticed your gun lying in the street."

"Is it okay?" Nightbreaker asked.

"It doesn't look dinged up, but I don't know what this thing is supposed to look like," the detective said. "But let's stay on the matter at hand."

Nightbreaker walked slowly towards his friend. There was still a throbbing in his head. "Who's next on the list?"

"Don't you think you should let us take care of this from now on?"

"Detective, you know you're not equipped to handle an extranormal criminal like this. You need me."

"Maybe you should call in your pals then."

"Not just yet," Nightbreaker said, his hand to his head. "I can't help thinking this is personal now."

Munchen frowned. "Before you go off on your personal mission, maybe you should rest. You don't look too good."

Nightbreaker straightened up. A police officer handed him the Multi-Gun. "On that, we agree."

"And you let me know what your next move is going to be, so you have back-up."

Nightbreaker nodded, an action that caused pain to explode in the back of his head. This was not his best showing.

• • •

He had driven slowly to his sanctum, careful lest he get into an accident. He was still woozy from the punishment he took from Flood. The Multi-Gun seemed fine, if scratched up. He hung it in its place on his tool board, followed by the line thrower. Nightbreaker undid his jacket and sat down in the nearest chair.

What had gone wrong? Obviously he had underestimated his foe; Flood had a great command of his powers, utilizing them as an expert. Nightbreaker wondered how a petty gunman gained these abilities, and how he gained the proficiency in using them.

But maybe this wasn't the time to ponder these things. Maybe it was time to go home to his wife and find some comfort there. He took off his kerchief and goggles and proceeded to transform from the heroic Nightbreaker to plain old Isaiah Copper.

There would be time to figure out how to overcome Flood tomorrow.

• • •

Isaiah woke to the smell of strong coffee. He rose from the bed he shared with his wife and put on his robe. Outside, the sky still had the rose-tinged shades of the dawn. He glanced at himself in the mirror; there was no bump, no bruise. From downstairs, his wife sang, a sweet noise to his ears.

He cinched the belt on the robe and moved forward out of the bedroom. As he got closer to the kitchen, new smells became apparent—bacon, scrapple. Isaiah assumed eggs were also in the offing, and his stomach growled in anticipation.

Isaiah smiled in spite of his dark mood once he saw his wife setting up a breakfast plate. Her brushfire red hair was still in early morning disarray. She hadn't put on her make-up yet, but it didn't detract from her beauty to him. She looked up and said, "Get over here and eat."

"Yes, ma'am," Isaiah responded and pulled a chair up to the table. He graciously accepted the plate piled high with food.

She stared at Isaiah for a moment. Her mouth compressed into a thin line. "I know that look. What's wrong?"

"What do you mean what's wrong?"

"I mean what's wrong. Something must have happened to you while you were out last night."

Isaiah sighed. One of the things that he was grateful for was how his wife Gloria knew his secret identity. It allowed him to open up fully to her. "Somebody died last night."

"I'm sure a lot of people died last night."

"This was somebody I was protecting. The man I was protecting him from overpowered me and succeeded in his mission."

"Oh, honey...."

"Gloria," Isaiah said. "This criminal...he had powers I don't know if I can overcome."

Gloria Copper put her hand over his. "Surely you must know that you can't save everyone."

"This is different. I was actively trying to prevent this man from dying, and I failed."

"You can't succeed every time, Isaiah Copper."

"I should have succeeded. I should have been ready for that monster and repelled him."

"Listen to me," she said, reaching out to stroke his cheek. "You cannot be ruled by these regrets. Mourn the man you failed to save, but use his memory to move you forward and help you bring this monster to justice."

He closed his eyes and kissed the palm of her hand. "I don't know if I can."

"If you can't, try harder. You need to put this murderer away, and only you can do it."

"You're too good to me."

"Oh, tell me something I don't know," Gloria shot back with a mocking smile. "Now finish your breakfast and get to work."

"Yes, ma'am."

• • •

Even with the pep talk from Gloria, the death of the tailor still nagged at Nightbreaker. As he stalked the Nocturne night, his mind dwelled on his confrontation with Flood. Surely, he reasoned, there was another way he could have handled the fight. Surely he could have saved the poor man.

Apparently Flood was going down the list of jurors in order, which was why he was wandering the edges of LaRouse, opposite a four story tenement building. The place had a newer sheen, part of the renovations that were making Nocturne into a better place. Nightbreaker wondered if this was where the young lady who judged Baker still lived. He had to assume that renovated apartment buildings were accompanied by raised rents. If the woman couldn't afford the new rate, she could be elsewhere.

Which might be why this building was the best place to confront Flood again.

This time, Nightbreaker had clued Munchen in on his plan. Below were a number of plainclothes officers, ready to spirit the woman away if Flood showed up. The other jurors were being located and put in protective custody. Nightbreaker hoped that Morai would be the last man killed by the water-controlling criminal. If he wasn't, the hero didn't know what he would do.

The walkie talkie clipped to his belt came alive. "Anything up there?"

Nightbreaker brought the unwieldy thing to his lips. "Nothing yet."

"Everything quiet down here," the plainclothesman below transmitted.

"Let us hope it remains as such."

The hero put back the walkie talkie and continued his vigil. He had already gotten his ally Ferryman to patrol Lincoln tonight. He had to entrust the vigilante with his home turf so he could concentrate on this situation. There would not be another death on his watch if he could help it.

The moon was high in the night sky. Clouds drifted across Nightbreaker's view. He paced around the roof, anxiously waiting for the villain to show himself. In his mind, he went through his last battle looking for some way he could have done things differently.

He waited one hour, two. It looked as if tonight would be a failure. He checked his Multi-Gun for what must have been the fifth time.

And then he saw it—a slight wavering of the horizon behind the tene-ment. Nightbreaker brought his weapon up, his mind working over what payload he should use. With his free hand he unclipped the walkie talkie. "He's coming."

"Right," the cop on the other end said, "We'll evacuate the target."

The wavering had risen. Nightbreaker could see the figure of Flood in the middle of the watery envelope that was now making its way across the rooftops. He switched out the walkie talkie for his line thrower and fired a strong cable across the street. Once more he swung out to deal with this liquid-based foe, trying hard not to think of his failure the last time they met.

Nightbreaker landed nimbly on the roof. In one smooth movement he stood up and unholstered his Multi-Gun. His thumb rotated the barrels looking for a proper payload.

The blue and yellow form of Flood approached rapidly. "You still won't give up," he said with a touch of mirth to his voice.

"No," Nightbreaker shot back.

"Then I guess I'll have to flatten you again, hero."

Flood motioned, sending out a jet of water. Nightbreaker dodged to the left, rolling on the roof's pebbled surface. Flood launched another stream, but he narrowly avoided it. In an instant, Nightbreaker let the mantra that kept him anchored to this reality go. Flood turned in his liquid cocoon, trying to figure out where the hero would manifest next.

Nightbreaker re-entered reality behind the stairway. He jumped out from his cover, his Multi-Gun in both hands. Quickly, he fired.

The payload entered the fluid corona surrounding Flood. There was a flash of light, a sizzling sound. The payload clattered to the floor. Flood was now on his back, struggling to breathe. Nightbreaker rushed over and straddled his foe. He pulled the man up by the collar. His uniform felt slick to the touch.

"Got you," the hero said.

Flood was taking in great gulps of air. His arm unsteadily moved to-ward the puddle surrounding the two. Without hesitation, Nightbreaker swung the Multi-Gun and fired. Flood found his arm affixed to the ground by ropes of a sticky adhesive. He altered his aim and fired another payload to tie down the other arm.

"They're not going to keep me long," Flood promised. "I'll escape and I'll get them all...then I'll come for you."

"You still won't give up."

"You're welcome to try," Nightbreaker replied as he reached for his walk-ie talkie. "Gentlemen, I have him."

And somehow, Nightbreaker thought that the fluid controlling miscreant was silently laughing at him.

• • •

The LaRouse Parish Police Precinct was smaller than Detective Munchen's home base of Jubilee's station. The lighting was dimmer, and the rooms sported details reaching back to the turn of the century. According to historians, the precinct was fashioned from a notorious bordello that was seized after years of catering to Nocturne's elite. The place still felt ancient in spite of the modern features it now sported.

Three officers had accompanied Flood to the holding cells. He was still wearing his uniform, his cowl pulled back and mask missing; once he was booked and sent to prison, he would be made to wear prison grays. There were four of the small concrete cells, thick iron bars designed to keep prisoners inside. There was a cot in one corner and a stained toilet in the back. A uniformed officer was left to serve as the guard, positioning himself at the door leading to the bullpen.

Flood sat down on the cot and stared at his new surroundings. In the next cell over, its inhabitant crooned softly. The villain looked at his bare hands. "Not going to happen again," he muttered to himself.

He got up and walked to the toilet. He looked down and slowly smiled. "I can work with this," he said.

• • •

Nightbreaker returned to his home late at night. The moon was slowly beginning to recede, letting dawn and daylight come forth. He snuck in carefully, slowly removing his uniform and placing the individual pieces on furniture across the rooms. There would be time to put the whole thing back in the closet tomorrow, he reasoned. He climbed the stairs to the bedroom and changed into his pajamas.

Gloria was still fast asleep in their bed, her eye-mask secure. Isaiah felt tired after confronting Flood. Truth was he felt he could sleep all day into the next night. But he was sure Detective Munchen would want a statement—maybe more—from him sometime during the day. He slipped under the covers and turned towards his wife. He took a moment to take in the woman's beauty and once more thanked God he somehow deserved her. Gloria shifted in her sleep and murmured something incoherent. He placed his arm around her.

Isaiah would still agonize over the death of that one former juror. He never was comfortable with people dying under his protection. But knowing that the man responsible was in custody and would face justice gave him some measure of solace. And that was enough to give him a dreamless sleep.

• • •

"Guard!"

Patrolman Lou Dinardo moved away from the door to the cell holding the water freak. He had his gun at the ready, prepared to plug him if he tried something.

Not that there ain't nothing he could try, Dinardo thought.

To his left, a pickpocket continued to protest his innocence. To his right, a man brought in on a drunk and disorderly was singing to himself. The water freak was at the bars, his bare hands at his sides.

"Whadda you want?" Dinardo sneered.

"I want out."

Dinardo adjusted his collar. "That's what everybody wants."

"But not everybody is like me," the water freak countered. "Let me show you."

Quickly, the water freak raised his arm. Behind him, a column of water rose from the toilet. Dinardo raised his gun, but before he could pull the trigger, the prisoner motioned with his hand. The column rushed towards Dinardo and surrounded his head. Water rushed into his nostrils and mouth. Dinardo shook his head, but the globe of liquid kept adhering to his head. Water rapidly filled his lungs. He began to convulse, his mouth opening involuntarily. Dinardo slowly slid down the wall as his vision dimmed.

And then patrolman Dinardo saw no more.

• • •

After breakfast, Isaiah Copper made his way to a boarded up gas station in Lincoln that hid his sanctum. He ducked under the boards that were nailed to the broken windows and through the garbage-strewn floor of what was once the cashier's office. He pushed aside a door hanging on one hinge and stepped onto the garage floor. Next to the door were two levers. Pulling the lever on the right caused a section of floor near the car bay open up, revealing a staircase leading down.

As he descended to the area he used as Nightbreaker's headquarters, Isaiah ruminated on what happened last night. The shock pack seemed to have worked well in stopping Flood. But he knew what happened—if he had been fully covered, there was a chance it wouldn't work. The possibility that he would have to face the demented young man again meant he would have to find another way to defeat him.

Isaiah went to one of the workbenches on the southern portion of the sanctum. He pulled open a drawer and removed a set of tools. Another drawer produced the payload shells he used in the Multi-Gun.

He wondered if he should call his friend Jenny Argo...maybe she could help him think of a new strategy to apply to Baker's superhuman alter-ego.

But he needed to come up with something quickly. He was not going to be caught unprepared again.

• • •

With a smirk, Flood allowed the water bubble that drowned the idiot cop to dissolve into a tiny torrent that flowed down the dead man's uniform. He mentally guided the stream across the uniformed policeman to focus on the keys on the man's belt. Flood increased the power of the flow, until the ring was pulled off the corpse. The keys fell to the floor, and Flood was already redirecting the water's direction and nature, turning the fluid into strong waves.

The keys slowly moved across the floor, propelled by the waves. The metal scraped wetly against the tiles. Once the ring bumped up against the bars, Flood reached through and grabbed the keys, hurriedly unlocking his cell while keeping an eye open for new arrivals.

He walked slowly across the floor, ignoring the pleas of other prisoners to be released. The water followed behind him in a liquid, pulsating mass. His eyes scanned his surroundings looking for the best way out. Obviously, going through the front door was problematic; it would lead to the station bullpen, and fighting the police alone was not appealing. There was a window at the opposite end of the corridor, but being on the third floor made getting to the ground a danger.

Except...

Flood turned and made for the window. As he passed each cell, he

motioned with his hand. From out of the toilets, columns of water spout-
ed, their trajectory altering until they joined the fluid following him. He
opened the window and looked out onto the street. There, at the edge of
the concrete street, was a fireplug. Flood smiled and reached out with his
power. In his mind, he envisioned the water held under pressure in the
fire plug. He concentrated on the fluid pressing against the cap, increasing
the force of the flow, encouraging the water pressure to increase. Beads of
sweat appeared on Flood's brow as he tried to bend the fluid to his will.

He could hear the metal strain. A rumble gave way to a shriek and
then the cap flew off the fire plug, letting out a torrent of water. Flood motioned with his hand, redirecting the flow towards the station and letting it
soar upwards until a powerful geyser was directly below him. He climbed
through the window. His heart pounded, wary about another policeman
walking in. Behind him, the prisoners begged to be taken along.

Carefully he stepped onto the waterspout. Liquid darkened his boots.
At first he struggled to balance on the powerful fountain, but managed to
keep himself upright. The villain reached out once again and willed the
spout to lower down to the ground. Above him, he could hear excited voices. He urged the liquid to lower himself quicker.

As he stepped off onto the ground, two policemen ducked their heads
out. "Hey, you!" called out one, a gaunt man with a thin mustache.

Flood motioned upwards with his arm. A powerful stream of water rose
up and blasted the two of them. He gathered up the rest of the water to re-
create the envelope he traveled in. As the fluid surrounded him, he began
to feel secure again.

A number of officers spilled out onto the street. Flood was ready for
them; even before they drew their weapons, he diverted a portion of fluid
and turned it into a powerful stream. The police found their feet knocked
out from under them. Flood moved quickly down the street. Ahead of him
was a manhole cover. He reached out for the water underneath and threw it
against the metal disc. The cover flew upwards, hit by a highly pressurized
stream of liquid. As the police officers came to their feet, Flood lowered
himself down the hole into the sewers.

By the time the patrolmen had gotten to the opening, Flood was gone.

• • •

The beautiful woman with short ice blonde hair nodded. "Could be
problematic."

"It's already proven to be," Isaiah said. He was leaning against a workbench on which was laid out a disassembled Multi-Gun and several pay-load shells. There was a distinct whiff of machine oil to the place right now. "I thought maybe a new set of eyes might help me come up with a new solution, Jenny."

While Isaiah had found he had a talent for science, Jennifer Argo was a genius in the field. Recently she had built a suit of powered armor that was taken over by a malevolent force before she could use it to be a hero. Her knowledge had fueled the success of her late father's company. If there was someone who could come up with an innovative way to capture Flood, it was her.

"The shock pack stopped him, you said."

"Once. He's not stupid. He'll be fully insulated next time, not partially."

Jenny stretched. Even though she appeared casual, dressed in a denim shirt, canvas pants and work boots, the sparkle in her light blue eyes made it clear she was excited by the prospect of a new situation to conquer. "If there is a next time. You said he was captured."

"Let's be serious," Isaiah said with a half smirk. "Even after dealing with special criminals for all these years, the Nocturne Police haven't adapted to dealing with them. Yes, there's a chance he won't get out, but there's a stronger chance he will."

"Well, let's hope they notify you if he does escape."

"They'll probably notify the remaining members of his jury first...and I'm worried they might not be able to protect them sufficiently."

"You think Flood's going to succeed?"

"It's a distinct possibility," Isaiah said. He picked up one of the payload shells. "I refuse to let him without a fight. I ended up allowing one person to die on his list; I won't go through it again."

Jenny nodded and rubbed her hands together. "Let's get started, then."

• • •

Flood emerged from the sewer a mile away from the police station. It was still dark out, with a moonless sky—the moon had set. A quick look about indicated he was in St. Carruthers, in the commercial district. He glided across the streets in his envelope of water, taking to the alleys and backways. He needed somewhere he could find a place to recuperate; rest and plan. He knew it was only a matter of time before news of his escape got to the ears of that infernal Nightbreaker, which meant he would have to overcome the hero to get to the other jurors.

There were several times when Flood had to hide like a scared little boy to avoid people discovering him. He hated having to do that, hated the feeling it engendered in him. With all this power, he should be sitting on a throne and luxuriating in the riches he was able to liberate from others. He shouldn't have to skulk about looking for a hole to crawl into.

Finally, he found an abandoned storefront near the train-yards. Flood utilized his powers to break down the boards blocking the entrance in a high-pressure stream of water. The place smelled of rat feces and mold, and the floor was strewn with garbage and broken pieces of furniture. He maneuvered his way carefully through the detritus and moved enough of the rubble out of the way to sit and contemplate his next move.

Flood sat in the dust and the dirt and tried to get some sleep. There would be much to do soon enough.

• • •

When Isaiah returned to his home, there was a note from his wife; Detective Munchen had called. Unmindful of the time, he headed for the phone in the living room and dialed his friend and ally. There were four rings before the detective picked up.

"Hello?" Munchen said on the other end of the line, sounding muzzy with sleep.

"It's Nightbreaker."

"Nightbrea—what in Sam Hill are you doing calling me this early? I still have three hours before I have to get up!"

Isaiah ignored the detective's annoyance. "Is it true? Flood is already back on the streets?"

Munchen sighed. "Yes. He staged a prison break in the middle of the night. Killed a police officer in the process. Wasn't easy breaking it to his widow."

"My sympathy," Isaiah said gently. "Any idea where he headed to?"

"No clue. Slippery skel ran out through the sewers. You could lose an elephant in that maze."

Isaiah bit back the urge to curse. He still wasn't ready, even if he had a possible solution to stop the miscreant. "Who's the next juror on his list?"

"Wilton Queen. He's a lawyer, specializes in corporate law. He just relocated his office to the edges of Silver Spire."

Isaiah looked for a piece of paper and a pencil. "Give me a moment," he told his friend until he found some. "Tell me his address."

Detective Munchen told him. Isaiah scribbled down the street and number.

"I'll visit him personally; try to get him to take a sudden vacation."

"Think he'll listen to a mystery man like you?"

"You know me by now. I can be persuasive when I want to be."

"I hope you can. I don't want any more bizarre drownings in my city."

"On that, my friend, we both agree," Isaiah said. "I'll contact you after I speak to Queen."

"Be careful."

"I plan on being."

• • •

Flood felt he was degrading himself. He had to drown a transient in a shallow puddle to steal his threadbare, dirty clothing. He donned the jacket, flannel shirt and pants frayed at the cuffs and went into town.

He needed to insulate himself, which meant gloves to match his suit. If it wasn't for his hands, after all, he would never have succumbed to Nightbreaker's electrical attack...and he wasn't going to fall for that again. Flood found a hardware store and roamed the corridors, eyes on the lookout for people. He located a pair of rubber work gloves and slid them into his jacket when no one was looking.

Flood skulked out of the store feeling like a common thief. This wasn't what he was given these abilities for. His powers were to elevate himself onto another plane, a place where no one could do anything to him again. His face flushed with shame as he stuck to the alleyways to make his way back.

When he was back in the abandoned storefront, he worked to modify his suit. Off in the distance, the sound of train whistles pierced the night. Flood remembered hearing the trains passing by the prison where he spent the last four years. He swore he wasn't going to sit in a cell hearing that sound again.

Flood finished his work. His mind was on Wilton Queen. It would be a matter of time before the fat little lawyer drowned in his liquid tide. And then he would finish off the others.

The sky was the limit after that.

• • •

Wilton Queen's office was right on the edge where white collar commercial buildings gave way to the factories and storage facilities that had been converted into homes for scientific concerns. It was in one of the more modern towers in the neighborhood, a monolith of glass and chrome that was topped with the silver spire from which the area now took its name.

Nightbreaker slipped into the building while out of phase with its reality. No one noticed him sliding past the security desk. He waited patiently for the elevator. Once inside, he briefly returned to this reality and pressed the button for the 12th floor where Queen held court

It was easy to find Queen's offices on the proper floor. The double glass doors displayed his name in a grand typeface. Nightbreaker mentally chanted the mantra that allowed him to stay in his old home dimension. The receptionist who was looking through the door dropped her pen, her mouth a little circle of surprise. Nightbreaker calmly walked into the office and acknowledged her reaction with a nod of his head.

"I'm here to see Mr. Queen," he told the attractive young woman.

For a second, the woman sat there frozen in her surprise; not sure of what to do. Then she rose and, still staring at him, went to the back. Meanwhile Nightbreaker took a seat in one of the straight-backed waiting room chairs. He waited, taking in the subdued, tasteful decor.

After five minutes, a corpulent, bespectacled man emerged from the back wearing a blue three piece suit. His black hair was slicked back, giving his face a blocky countenance. The glasses were so thick they reduced his pupils to pinpoints. He took a position directly in front of Nightbreaker, thumbs hooked in his vest.

"You gave my receptionist quite the fright."

Nightbreaker rose and extended his hand. Queen did not take it. "I'm sorry, but there's an urgency to my needing to see you."

"Well, Mr. Nightbreaker—you're seeing me, so state your piece."

"Do you remember someone named Scott Baker?"

"The name doesn't ring any bells."

"Well, you should remember him," Nightbreaker said. "You sent him to prison."

"You have the wrong man. I'm in patent law, not criminal prosecution."

"No, but you were on the jury that convicted Baker. He's out, and he has powers, and he's looking to kill you and the other jurors."

"If he's looking for revenge, why go after us? Why not the judges, the lawyers."

"Because you and your fellows were the ones who sealed his fate."

Queen shrugged. "Fine. If he's a super-freak, aren't you and your kind responsible for keeping him from hurting normal people like me?"

Nightbreaker kept quiet. The words surprised and stung him. It wasn't long ago that he hid his heritage to avoid being referred to as "your kind." After he got over the hurt, Nightbreaker said, "We think you're next."

"We? You mean your Shadow Legion friends?"

"I have a relationship with the NPD. I've been working with them to keep you and the other jurors safe."

"And how has that worked out?" Queen asked with a sneer in his voice.

"You're not a pleasant man," Nightbreaker observed. Behind his goggles, his eyes narrowed.

"I'm not paid to be pleasant."

Nightbreaker paused. "We're going to keep you safe. I will keep you safe, regardless of how you treat me. Still, you should look over your shoulder from time to time."

Queen nodded. "I'll remember that."

"If you see anything that might indicate Baker's close, contact Detective Munchen. He'll most likely give you a visit later."

"And you just figured you'd do your visiting first."

"Be careful, Mr. Queen," Nightbreaker said as he turned to leave.

• • •

Nightbreaker sat in his Jaguar and struggled with his frustration. It was not just because Queen was arrogant in his rejection. He knew Flood was out there, ready to continue his vendetta. And there was no doubt he needed to be stopped before there was more death on his hands.

There was also the problem of the Nocturne Police. Flood had killed one of their own; the desire for the criminal's blood would be great amongst the dead man's fellows. It was not Flood's life he feared for, but the potential for more policemen to fall that worried him.

Nightbreaker headed towards Lincoln, thoughts of his latest work crawling into his mind. He worried that the new payload he and Jenny Argo had conceived of wouldn't be ready. If it wasn't, there was nothing to stop Flood.

And that was something Nightbreaker couldn't live with.

• • •

Wilton Queen watched the vigilante drive off from his window. His face was flush red with anger. How dare this Nightbreaker dictate to him about some super-freak hunting him. The truth was Wilton hated how these super-powered idiots were proliferating in his city. There was no room for people who could fly and disappear at will in his vision for Nocturne.

So he was in the crosshairs from this Baker person, was he? He had connections; it would take only a few phone calls to get himself a top notch security detail. Let this Baker super-freak come after him. Wilton didn't care what he could do—it'd be hard to kill him if this creep was riddled with bullets.

Wilton went back to his office. He began to resent Nightbreaker more for taking him away from his work. There were a number of cases that required his attention today, and he spent time he didn't have talking to the so-called mystery man. Who knew how long it would take for him to catch up.

He took the spectacles out of his pocket and placed them on his nose. With a slight grunt borne of the creaky limbs brought on by age, Wilton lowered himself into his brand new wingback chair. He picked up the manila folder that was lying on the pristine blotter on top of his sleek, modern desk.

Before he could start reviewing the briefs, Wilton heard a curious sound. He put down the folder and spun in his chair.

Behind him, the floor to ceiling glass windows that afforded him a sterling view of the beautiful technological businesses of Silver Spire were covered in a flowing sheet of water. Wilton rose, confusion in his mind. When he was in the reception area, it was sunny and dry; judging from the way the water was pouring down the surface, it was a downpour. Something was wrong.

Wilton jumped when the glass buckled, its once pristine appearance now marred by a spider web of cracks.

"What the...?" the lawyer asked.

It was the last thing he said before the torrent of water rushed in.

• • •

Nightbreaker heard the distinct, distant sound of shattering glass. He looked up to see something slithering in a jagged hole, something fluid. He quickly got out of his car and ran back, his hand unclipping his line thrower. In one smooth motion, he brought the device up and fired. A thin,

Wilton hated how these super-powered idiots were proliferating in his city.

strong cable arced into the air and attached itself to the building. Night-breaker flicked a switch. With a whisper-quiet whirr, the line was rolled back into the thrower, lifting him up towards the hole.

Once he was up to the floor where Wilton Queen had his offices, Night-breaker saw Flood standing over Queen, water engulfing the portly lawyer. He landed on the floor, Multi-Gun at the ready, and called out, "Let him go!"

"I'd rather let him die," the villain shot back.

Noticing that Flood was without his fluid envelope, Nightbreaker quick-ly thumbed the dial on his signature weapon. He fired a payload. The small circular object hit Flood square in the chest, knocking the criminal back as if hit by a cannonball. The water surrounding Queen sloughed off him.

Good. He has to concentrate to keep up his water constructs.

"Get out of here!" he said sharply to Queen, who was sputtering and spitting out water. The man got to his feet and headed for the reception area, each step making a tiny splash.

Flood was slowly rising. "You shouldn't have done that."

Nightbreaker shot another impact payload at Flood. "I won't let you kill again!"

The villain slammed into the wall from the power of the payload. Al-ready, the water on the floor was being gathered about Flood. "He deserves to die!"

"Because he sent you to prison?"

"Because he took my life!"

A stream of water rose up from Nightbreaker's feet and hit him in the face, knocking him back. The hero struggled to stay on his feet, all too aware of the sheer drop at his back. Flood moved forward, his water en-velope now fully surrounding him. Nightbreaker changed the setting on his Multi-Gun for shock payloads and fired. The villain did not seem to be affected.

"I'm not stupid," he said to the hero. "I insulated myself this time."

"Should've known." Nightbreaker took a deep breath and charged the miscreant, breaking through the water wall and wrapping his arms around Flood's waist. The two went though the envelope of fluid and hit the floor. The water once more crashed to the floor as Nightbreaker hit his quarry as hard as he could. Flood returned the blows, and the two rolled about the now sodden carpeted floor. The villain managed to get a foot under Night-breaker. He pushed, knocking the hero off of him. Nightbreaker fell flat on his back. Flood got to his feet and motioned with his hand. The water rose and fell upon the hero in a powerful deluge that pushed Nightbreaker back and out of the building.

Nightbreaker fell quickly. He grabbed his line thrower and fired, sending a piton towards the roof. Flood flowed out of the hole in the glass, sliding down the outer wall with an effortless grace. The line grew taut, and Nightbreaker swung toward the building. By the time his feet touched the edifice's surface, Flood had already reached the ground and was retreating.

Nightbreaker slowly lowered himself down to the street.

And he was smiling.

• • •

He sped to his sanctum and called Jenny Argo. "Are they ready?"

"As it's ever going to be."

"Good. I'll come over and pick them up. I know where this snake is."

"How?"

Nightbreaker went over to a small console in a corner of his workshop. He flicked a switch. The viewscreen came alive, an illuminated line sweeping in a circular path. At one point, there was a blip. "I laid one of the tracking devices you developed for me on him."

"So it's working?"

"So far. It'll only be a matter of time before I get him."

"Hopefully before he kills anyone."

"This man won't kill anyone again," Nightbreaker said grimly. "I swear it."

• • •

Fury filled Flood's mind. He stalked around the abandoned storefront, kicking at the debris at his feet. A rat squeaked as a stray rock hit it. The wind whistled through the spaces between the masonry.

That idiot Nightbreaker had denied him again. He had the fat little lawyer in his grip—was watching him drown—and this so-called hero messed it up. Now he was back at the beginning. Only now the lawyer was aware of him. For all he knew, his roly-poly quarry was even now leaving the city until it all blew over.

Things were closing in on him. The police were obviously looking for him, anxious to avenge the death of that stupid cop. Nightbreaker, it seemed, wasn't going to give up. And the jurors who sent him away were all aware that he was coming. But the fear he was hoping to instill in them was most likely replaced by hope that they would be protected.

Flood had to change that, and change it quickly. He had to have his vengeance before he could move forward as a villain, as a veritable *super*villain. There were so many things he knew he could do with these new powers.

But he *had* to put Nightbreaker down. Soon.

• • •

Nightbreaker slid the payload shells into his Multi-Gun. Each one of the disc-like objects settled into the muzzle with a quiet click. He brought the weapon to his eye to check the sightlines.

"You sure these are going to work."

The beautiful blonde scientist shrugged. "You should know by now there's never 'sure' in science. But I'm willing to guess the percentage of it working as we thought is pretty high."

Nightbreaker put the Multi-Gun into its specialized holster. "Let's hope so."

"What are you planning on doing?" Jenny Argo asked.

"The tracer is working like a dream."

"Thank you."

"And I'm going to find that lowlife and finally bring him in for good."

Nightbreaker moved toward the door. Jenny leaned against the simple, utilitarian chair in her workshop. "I suppose I should wish you luck."

"And I suppose I should thank you."

"You're welcome."

"And if I don't come back in about an hour, hour and a half," Nightbreaker said, "Contact the others."

He didn't have to say who the others were; Jenny had already met with his teammates in the Shadow Legion. He knew she didn't approve of them, but he hoped that she respected them.

"I will," she said.

And Nightbreaker left Jenny's workshop to meet with Flood for what he hoped would be the last time.

• • •

The two story building looked like many of the buildings in Carruthers—decaying, dingy and devoid of life. Ever since manufacturing started leaving Nocturne for greener fields, the neighborhood had decayed into something resembling his childhood home in Lincoln. The only difference, it seemed, was in the color of the resident's skin. The cloudy night sky only contributed to the oppressive nature of the place.

The blip was on the center of the viewscreen, meaning Flood was in that building. The sign on the begrimed storefront advertised it being a hardware store; Nightbreaker wondered who the proprietor was and why he had to close the place. He got out of the black Jaguar and pulled up the kerchief to fully slip into his identity. The Multi-Gun was heavy on his hip. Nightbreaker took a deep breath and walked inside.

The insides of the store were oppressively quiet save for the chittering of vermin. He unclipped a small handheld torchlight Jenny had made for him and flicked it on. A bright beam revealed aisles of wooden shelves, some buckling under the weight of time. The floor was littered with scattered nuts, bolts and nails. Signs advertising tools and paint were faded with age. The smell was of garbage and decay. A rat ran across the floor quickly. It was hard to imagine this place as a vital business.

Nightbreaker swept the torchlight from left to right, his eyes behind his goggles struggling to adjust to the darkness. "I know you're in here," he muttered.

• • •

Flood watched through a jagged hole in the second floor of the store. His enemy had arrived. Anger welled up deep inside him, a desire to crush him once and for all. There was one problem...

Water was sparse.

There were some slight puddles on this floor, but not enough to use against this Nightbreaker effectively. He could sense a water main deep below the storefront, but the layers of concrete and tightly packed dirt made it impossible to access it. He was now effectively just a man in a suit, which meant the hero would have an advantage with his powers and gun.

Behind him, lightning flashed. Flood turned his head in the direction of the second-quick radiance. In the time he took a breath, thunder rumbled loudly. He caught a whiff of ozone...

And the sky opened up. Rain began to fall.

Flood smiled.

• • •

Nightbreaker ignored the lightning arcing across the sky. He paid no mind to the angry thunderclap.

But when he heard the pitter-patter of raindrops falling on the roof and the street outside, he felt a chill run down his spine. He lowered the torchlight. Behind his goggles, he looked for a way out.

Behind him he heard the creak of straining wood. In a split second, the creak gave way to the rifle shot of boards used to cover the windows of this abandoned store being reduced to splinters. Nightbreaker turned, his hand reaching for his Multi-Gun, to see a powerful stream of water barreling towards him. He loosened his muscles, went limp as the beam of concentrated raindrops slammed into him. It forced him back into the wall with such force that it caused the substandard sheetrock to buckle and break.

Nightbreaker took in a deep breath as the sudden stream dissipated. The torchlight had been knocked out of his hands and was now being carried away by a rapidly running string of liquid. He pushed off from the cracked and crumbling wall. Murky light was streaming in from outside and Nightbreaker's eyes struggled to adjust to the change in illumination.

Flood lowered himself on a column of rainwater. Nightbreaker drew his weapon, but the villain motioned with his hand, sending a high pressure deluge to knock the Multi-Gun away.

"If you were going to live long enough," Flood said triumphantly, "you'd regret coming out here tonight."

"I regret having to hear you ramble on," Nightbreaker shot back. Already, Flood was constructing the envelope of water he surrounded himself with so he could travel. The fluid was up to his knees.

Flood motioned again, sending a stream of water screaming towards Nightbreaker's head. The hero fell into a crouch, avoiding the blast. He glanced about hurriedly looking for his weapon. The Multi-Gun was now behind him. Hurriedly, he slipped into his sidereal dimension and dove for the many-barreled pistol. The minute his fingers fell on the butt of the gun, he re-entered his base reality, rolling into a crouch and firing a payload at his enemy.

The water envelope was now almost complete. Flood twisted in the fluid, causing the front of the envelope to extend outwards. The payload hit the water and slowed the projectile until it floated lazily. Flood raised his hand, and the fluid rose sinuously, dropping the circular object to the floor.

"I'm not going to allow you to knock me around again," Flood said and sent another powerful stream at the hero. Nightbreaker dove, but was hit in the leg. He spun around and fell to the hardwood floor. The impact of the blast knocked the air out of his lungs. He struggled to breathe, aware of the water rising up from the floor. He once more slipped between dimensions just as the fluid dove for the spot where his head was. Nightbreaker rose, checked the Multi-Gun and ran to a position right behind Flood. He re-entered his base reality and grabbed a dowel, swinging at Flood's head with all his might. Flood moved to the right; the dowel broke in two over the villain's shoulder. Nightbreaker rose his weapon and fired, the payload knocking Flood out of his envelope. Flood hit a shelving unit and shook his head. The envelope hit the floor with a splash.

Flood motioned, and the water running along the floor began to run up Nightbreaker's body. The hero traversed dimensions again and stepped out of the path of the advancing fluid. He moved to the left, thumbing the barrels of the Multi-Gun. When he re-entered the base dimension, Flood was already there. The villain blasted him into one of the shelving units. The shelves teetered and fell on top of Nightbreaker with a crash. Nightbreaker's muscles strained to lift the heavy piece of furniture on top of him. He could hear the *shurring* of Flood advancing on him.

It was obvious time was running out. Nightbreaker was sure he couldn't get out from under the shelving before Flood attacked. He twisted his torso until he could face the villain. Flood was almost right on top of him. Nightbreaker brought his Multi-Gun up and fired a payload.

Flood laughed. "You know that won't work..."

The fluid using criminal's attention was drawn to the bottom of the water envelope. Something was swirling in the miniature currents, a dark crimson cloud that was spreading. Nightbreaker shot again, this payload hitting Flood in the chest. A second cloud of red bloomed from the circular payload. Flood suddenly stopped moving as a portion of the cloud seemed to solidify.

"What is this?" he cried out.

"It's a special compound I devised with a friend of mine," Nightbreaker explained. "A sort of quick setting gelatin. It'll hold you fast once it dissolves, but it's porous enough you'll still be able to breathe."

The red cloud spread out in the envelope and darkened into the solid gelatin. Flood struggled to move only to find himself held fast in the sticky red material. After a moment, the villain screamed in frustration.

"Can I take that to mean you give up?" Nightbreaker asked.

The glare coming from the eyes behind the mask spoke volumes.

• • •

It took a while, but Nightbreaker finally extricated himself from the buckling shelving. Flood was immobile save for his eyes, keeping sight of the hero with murderous intent. Nightbreaker dusted himself off and headed out to the street to find a phone booth. When he returned, he told Flood, "The police are on their way...and this time they won't be as careless with you as they were last time."

"I'm going to kill you," Flood hissed.

"A lot of people have tried, and yet I'm still here."

"I can be persistent."

"You've proved that to me."

"You're going to be dead."

"We're all going to be dead. I just don't plan on it anytime soon."

Nightbreaker could hear sirens in the distance. He scanned the store for a less obvious exit than the front door. There was another door in the back; it wouldn't take much exertion to break through. He smiled underneath his bandana. "That's the trash pick up. I'll leave you to them."

"This is not over," Flood said. "Not by half."

"When you're ready," Nightbreaker replied, "I'll be here."

• • •

The police had shown him the device under Flood's costume, a sort of harness with a wave sigil in its center. Nightbreaker placed a call to Jenny Argo to help him examine the curious device. The police had agreed to let the two examine the harness in a special room in the mortician's offices.

Nightbreaker watched as his beautiful friend first dismantled, then prodded Flood's mechanism for a half hour. He occasionally handed her a tool she required, but mainly he was a witness to the proceedings.

When she was done, Jenny wiped some sweat from her brow. "This...is unlike anything I've ever seen before."

"Jenny, you've seen everything."

"Not this. The circuitry is very advanced. I notice some similarities with Professor Ybarri's Brain-Machine Interface, some control elements like the ones coming out of one of the technological firms, but not in these configurations."

"I am just surprised no one noticed he was wearing this under his costume."

Jenny looked towards her friend and ally. "And he used this to mentally control water?"

Nightbreaker nodded. "It behaved as if it were alive."

"We need to find out who put this together. If more of this technology gets into hands like his—"

"It'll be chaos in the streets," the hero answered. "Trust me, I know."

• • •

Nightbreaker, in his identity of Isaiah Copper, walked through the grounds of Bailey Cemetery. His wife was at his side, her arm entwined with his. The green grass surrounding them seemed vivid in contrast to the grey gravestones going back over a hundred years. Some of the stones were so old their inscriptions had been almost totally worn away. Gnarled trees threw long shadows on the ground. The couple walked passed the bronze statue honoring the military dead until they came to a newer headstone.

The headstone said 'Morai' and gave the years of the man's life. The ground before the stone had the marks of being newly turned. Isaiah stood before the grave and lowered his head, a prayer on his lips.

When he was done, he said, "This is my fault."

"Hush, Isaiah Copper," his wife said, rubbing his arm with her delicate hand. "You couldn't have known what you were up against at that time."

"It doesn't matter." Isaiah touched the top of the headstone. "The people of this city, they count on me to save them from menaces like Flood. I can't afford to be taken by surprise. I can't afford to make a mistake like this."

"We're all going to make mistakes, and we're all going to lose people. The best we can do is make sure there is as little misfortune as possible."

"Even losing one life is too many. I swear I won't let this happen again."

Well, whatever you dedicate yourself to, I'll be there supporting you." Gloria reached up and kissed Isaiah on the cheek. "I love you."

"I love you, too." Isaiah turned away from the gravestone. "But I'm not going to forget this man, and I'm going to do my best to keep others from following him to this place."

The couple left the simple slab of stone, lost in their own thoughts. And somewhere, the wind whispered through the trees, seeming to send their encouragement.

THE END

THOMAS DEJA - has been writing professionally for almost twenty five years. Starting with a column and random horror serials in the seminal Brooklyn 'zine *Inside Joke*, Thomas began placing stories in such independent magazines as *After Hours* and *Not One of Us* before becoming one of the contributing book reviewers and feature writers for *Fangoria* magazine, a position he kept for over fifteen years. He wrote stories featuring classic Marvel Super-heroes for such anthologies as *The Ultimate Hulk* and *Five Decades of The X-Men*. Recently, he had become known for writing stories in what he calls The Chimera Falls Universe, including tales in both editions of *How The West Was Weird*, and the Shadow Legion series, starting with *New Roads To Hell*. Along with his best friend Derrick Ferguson, Thomas co-hosts *Better In The Dark*, a (more or less) bi-weekly movie podcast. Thomas' passion for film has extended to maintaining *Damn Your Ears! Damn Your Eyes!*, a blog where he publishes his notorious '10 Statements About' kinda, sorta movie reviews. A lifelong Jets fan, he also writes and podcasts about football for Tricycleoffense.com. Thomas lives in New York City, something he hopes to rectify soon.

People who are interested in learning more about the Chimera Falls Universe are invited to visit The Nocturne Travel Agency at http://welcometonocturne.blogspot.com/

THE DEATH RAY
(A DOC ATLAS ADVENTURE)

By Michael A. Black & Ray Lovato

September 5, 1946
New York Harbor

The bright lights of the cityscape shone against a black velvet sky and were reflected upon the dark water, which undulated against the seemingly endless rows of moored ships and boats. The two uniformed policemen strolled along the dock and one of them turned up his collar to stave off the evening chill, even though it was an early autumn night. The other copper snorted a laugh.

"Murph, you gotta be part reptile. How can you be getting cold on a beautiful night like this?"

Murphy tightened the jacket around his slender frame and frowned. "Guess I don't have as much meat on my bones as you do, O'Hara."

O'Hara laughed. "Let's wander down a bit more to the next call-box. I got me a hunch that St. Michael might have left us a little something to make the night go faster."

Murphy looked at his partner and grinned. "I'm all for that."

The two coppers quickened their pace. Murphy looked around warily.

"You got any chewing gum? You don't suppose Lieutenant Muldoon will happen down this way, do you?" He repeated his wary scanning of the area. "It wouldn't do for him to catch us."

"Muldoon's probably got a load on himself. He was laughing and joking about the brass being nervous about this ridiculous threat about blowing something up." They got to the callbox and he took out his key and inserted it into the slot.

"You think it's a phony?"

O'Hara frowned and pulled open the front of the iron callbox and retrieved the metal flask. He twisted the cap off and licked his lips.

"Well?" Murphy asked. "Do you?"

"Do I what?" O'Hara covered his badge with his left hand and brought the half-pint bottle up to his lips to take a long pull. He lowered the bottle and emitted a satisfied sigh, his breath redolent with the smell of fine whiskey.

"I'm forgetting me manners." He handed the bottle to Murphy, who wiped off the top with his palm and then took a few quick slugs. When he lowered the bottle his mouth twisted into a simper.

"The Lord be praised," he said. "Is that Powers?"

"Would a good Irishman be offering anything less?"

They each took a few more sips and then O'Hara screwed the cap back on. "Always best to keep a little in the can."

Murphy nodded and glanced around again. "Good thinking. We do have to keep on the watch till the wee hours." He clicked his tongue. "So what's your opinion of this death ray threat?"

O'Hara started to set the bottle back in the recesses of the call box, then hesitated, unscrewing the cap once more. "Well, I think it's a testament to the stupidity of the brass that they'd let a recorded threat from some nincompoop, calling himself *The Dark Destroyer*, and saying how he's gonna blow up something on these here docks, using some kind of ray gun from a Flash Gordon movie, disturb the goings on of the regular patrol beats in this, the finest city in the world—next to Dublin, that is. They must be candidates for the looney bin." He grinned. "But who am I to complain?" he said, taking another long drink from the bottle. "We're making a nickel or two for doing next to nothing."

Murphy slapped him and motioned for a turn. O'Hara nodded and handed it over, emitting a loud belch.

"Damn," Murphy said. "That one was so loud, they probably heard it all the way back at headquarters." He took another quick sip. "But what if this Destroyer bloke does have some kind of death ray?"

"Flash Gordon must've given it to him." O'Hara laughed and reached for the bottle when something stopped him. "You hear that?"

"What?"

Perhaps one hundred yards from the docks a lighted cabin cruiser sounded its horn as it proceeded toward the mouth of the Hudson.

"That boat," O'Hara said. "Like it was signaling us, or something."

Just then the high-pitched whine of a speed boat's motor sliced through the night. Both men hurried to the end of the pier and glanced out on the water. The darkness was so pervasive that no other craft could be discerned, but the sound was growing unmistakably closer. Suddenly a bright light illuminated about fifty yards behind the cabin cruiser. A bright, glowing beam of light shot across the surface of the water toward the cabin cruiser. The beam seemed to grow in intensity and concentrated on the boat, and an eerie sound, like a siren's wail, began shrieking along the surface of the water.

"What in blazes—" O'Hara started to say, when an explosive blast tore through the night and the subsequent concussive blast knocked both policemen off their feet.

Murphy was the first to recover, rolling onto his stomach and staring over at the orange glow of a dozen or so floating pools of fire floated on the surface of the water where the cabin cruiser had been. The powerful beam of light had disappeared.

"Sweet mother of Mary," Murphy said. He glanced back toward the open water but saw only darkness along with the fading sound of the speedboat's motor.

• • •

Thomas "Mad Dog" Deagan sat puffing on his cigar on the 88th floor of the Empire State Building, the recently established headquarters for Atlas Industries, as he perused the story of the previous night's explosion that was on the front page of the New York Daily News. The headline was ominous:

DEATH RAY SINKS SHIP

Although city officials were quick to attribute the explosion to an unfortunate accident that is under investigation, an exclusive account from two New York City Police Officers who witnessed the event at the scene stated that the destruction was caused by a death ray that was focused on the unfortunate boat. Sources confirmed that the there was an extra police presence on the docks last night, but denied that anything untoward was suspected. Unnamed sources from within the police department, however, hinted that a threat was received several days ago stating that a boat was going to be destroyed as a demonstration of power. These sources also suggested that this threat, which was in the form of a recorded message, specified that more destruction would be imminent if certain demands were not met. There is no further information available regarding the extent of the demands, but the anonymous sender identified himself as The Dark Destroyer.

A signal bell chimed and Deagan lowered the paper. He got up and glanced toward the hallway that led to the office area. The door to Doc's office was still closed. He took another long drag on the cigar and scrutinized the closed-circuit television monitor that showed who was ascending in the specially equipped elevator to this 88th floor level. Deagan immediately recognized the debonair figure of Edward "Ace" Assante. The man always dressed in impeccably tailored suits and was a dead ringer for actor Errol Flynn. Deagan, on the other hand, could barely find clothes that fit his ungainly, but muscular frame. He decided to have a bit of fun and drew in a prodigious amount of smoke from the stogie as he walked through the foyer area that was still under construction and positioned himself in front of the elevator doors. He waited, knowing the elevator had an automated function that only allowed it to stop at the 87th and 88th floors of the building. A special key was required to gain access to the elevator, and Doc Atlas had been very selective as to whom those keys were given. Deagan had one, as did Assante, but that was it, with the exception of the newly hired chief secretary, Polly St. Claire, who was in charge of supervising the massive office staff that Doc had recently hired.

Polly St. Clair, Deagan thought. *Now she was somebody he wouldn't mind getting next to on a tunnel of love ride at Coney Island sometime.*

The smoke was burning the inside of Deagan's mouth and throat and he considered exhaling, but the temptation to blow the noxious cloud directly into Assante's face as he exited the elevator was too much of a temptation. While he secretly liked and admired Ace, Deagan felt in constant competition with the man. When Deagan had retired from the Army as a Lieutenant Colonel, he was hired by Doc Atlas as a sort of trouble shooting foreman for Atlas Industries. Doc had also retained the services of Assante's legal expertise. During their military years, Deagan had outranked both Doc and Assante, who Deagan reluctantly admitted was probably the best pilot he knew, next to Doc. Dr. Michael Atlas seemed to be the best at everything, and proved it by performing special commando raids during the war, oftentimes being dropped behind enemy lines. A virtual superman, he was the greatest soldier Deagan had ever seen. The greatest man as well. Both he and Assante had accompanied Doc on numerous missions, and Deagan couldn't have been prouder when he'd been asked to associate himself with the man who had come to be known as The Golden Avenger.

Deagan closed his eyes, concentrating on not expelling the cigar smoke in an overdue cough, and finally heard the elevator come to a stop at this level. Puffing his cheeks out, he waited a few seconds more, the tears forming behind his closed eyelids and beginning to run down his cheeks.

The doors opened and Deagan let go with a hearty cough, spewing an effluvium of smoke-laden air.

But instead Ace's voice a feminine cry erupted. Deagan opened his eyes and saw Polly St. Claire in the midst of a coughing fit, waving her hand in front of her face. Assante gripped her elbow and glared at Deagan.

"Polly?" Deagan said, "How'd you get on the elevator?"

"You idiot," Ace said. "She got on as I was coming up."

"Aww, gee, I didn't know." Deagan's face crinkled like wrinkled paper. "I'm sorry."

Polly, her blue eyes still filled with tears, her red hair hanging over her shoulders in a brilliant cascade, tried to say something, but it was smothered by more coughing. Ace helped her out of the elevator and over to a nearby chair. He walked slowly, his right hand gripping the handle of an ornate cane.

"I didn't mean for you to be there," Deagan said. "I thought it would be Ace."

Assante frowned and waved his hat at the still smoldering cigar. "May I suggest you find and appropriate place to store that? You know how Doc frowns upon tobacco use in his presence."

Deagan's mouth tugged into a defiant expression, but before he could speak Polly nodded her head.

"Yes," she managed to say, still gasping. "Please get rid of that thing."

"Aww, Polly, I'm sorry." Deagan lifted his foot up and stubbed the cigar out on the sole of his shoe.

She stood up and headed toward the elevator. "I need to go to the ladies room."

"Wait," Deagan said. "Are you okay? You need any help?"

Polly turned her head and glared at him, then stuck the key into the slot. The elevator doors opened and she got on. "Tell Doc someone is bringing over the newspaper files he wanted." She brought her hand to her mouth and resumed coughing as the door slid closed.

Ace had a smile as wide as a city block on his face. "Does she need any help in the ladies room?" He laughed out loud and poked Deagan's rump with the cane. "Swell move, Romeo. Isn't she the girl you've been pining over the past few weeks?"

Deagan's big fingers crushed the cigar to brown pulp. "You shoulda' let me know she was on that elevator, dammit."

Ace laughed. "Any time you want some lessons on dealing with the fairer sex, let me know."

The door to Doc's office opened and three men stepped out. Two were rather average looking men in suits. The third was Doc Atlas. His light brown hair was still cut military-short, and the loose fitting double-breasted jacket he wore could hardly conceal the immensity of his frame. Even in normal business attire he exuded a sense of power and authority. His handsome, chiseled features exhibited no surprise at seeing Ace standing there with Deagan.

"Gentlemen," Doc said. "May I present my two associates, Misters Assante and Deagan." He extended his hand toward the pair that had left his office. "These are Special Agents Dexter Pauls and Arthur Smith of the Federal Bureau of Investigation."

The men shook hands all around as the standard greetings were exchanged.

The man called Smith eyed both Deagan and Ace before turning back to Doc. "We appreciate your time, Dr. Atlas. And as we said, it would be greatly appreciated by Washington if you would keep this matter in the strictest confidence." He was a big man, almost as big as Doc, with a pasty complexion and very short, blond hair with the exception of a longer section at the peak. The other man, Pauls, was short and swarthy, and had a face like a weasel.

Doc merely nodded. "Thomas, if you'd be good enough to show these gentlemen to the elevator."

"Sure," Deagan said. "This way guys."

Doc's nostrils twitched slightly. "Has someone been smoking?"

"Your new chief secretary just left," Ace said, shooting a grin at Deagan.

Deagan glared back at him.

"Miss St. Clair doesn't smoke," Doc said.

Ace shrugged. "She sure was smoking when she left."

Doc's eyes flicked toward both of them, then he turned and began walking back toward the offices. "Meet me in the library. Thomas, bring me the newspaper."

Deagan and Assante exchanged a quick look, both knowing that something was up. Deagan motioned for Smith and Pauls to follow him and summoned the elevator with the special key. Once it arrived, he reached inside and pressed the button for the ground floor. The two government men got on and the doors closed behind them.

"I wonder what that was all about?" Deagan said.

Ace shrugged and walked toward the library. "I would imagine we're about to find out."

Stacks of books that had yet to be sorted sat on the long, mahogany table inside the library. Doc stood near the front of the room where a portable chalkboard had been placed. Deagan and Ace sat in two of the empty chairs near the door.

"Doc," Deagan said. "About that smoking incident earlier—"

Doc Atlas raised his hand in a dismissive gesture. "We have more important matters to discuss, gentlemen. Ace, do you have any significant plans for the next few days?"

Ace removed a blue, pocket-sized appointment book from his jacket pocket and paged through it. "A few insignificant court appearances that any of my father's associates can handle."

Doc nodded slightly. "And Thomas, I'm sure that your schedule is open as well?"

"Of course, Doc. All I been doing is supervising the remodeling of this place. And trying to sort through your mountain of books."

"Need me to write down the alphabet for you?" Ace said.

Deagan frowned. "Need me to underline that line in Shakespeare's play where he talks about killing all the lawyers?"

Doc cleared his throat and strode forward, picking up the newspaper and pointing to the front page. "Need I remind you we have some special business to look into?"

Ace leaned forward. "That absurd headline about a death ray? What new lows will they sink to?"

"I don't know," Deagan said. "I kinda got a kick out of it. Reminded me of an old Flash Gordon movie. The Dark Destroyer... Like Ming, the Merciless."

"Nonetheless," Doc said, "a pleasure craft was destroyed last night in the harbor, ostensibly because the extortive demand was not met."

"Extortion?" Ace asked.

"The wire recording device that was delivered to the mayor's office a few days ago," Doc said. "A person identifying himself as the Dark Destroyer demanded five hundred thousand dollars be paid to him, lest he unleash the death ray and destroy a ship or boat."

Ace's eyes narrowed a bit. "Doc, was that what those two government men were here about?"

Doc's nod was fractional. He rarely wasted more motion than was necessary.

"They were questioning me about an examination I made of some papers and notebooks that had belonged to Nikola Tesla."

"Tesla?" Ace said. "Wasn't he some kind of crackpot?"

"He had some innovative ideas," Doc said. "Alternating current and early wireless communication. Unfortunately, many of them were closer to Jules Verne than Albert Einstein."

"A death ray," Deagan said. "The Dark Destroyer... Like I said, pure Flash Gordon stuff."

"To the best of my recollection," Ace said. "Tesla died back a few years ago."

"Nineteen forty-two, to be exact," Doc said. "Due to his reputation as an innovator and inventor, his papers and notebooks were confiscated by the FBI after his death, and eventually turned over to the Department of the Navy. The man had no known heirs."

"When did you review the stuff?" Deagan asked. "To the best of *my* recollection, we were all in the service after Pearl Harbor, and overseas for most of the next four."

"I was assigned to temporary duty back here in Washington for about two weeks," Doc said. "During that time, another scientist and I went through Tesla's papers."

"Did you find the death ray stuff?" Deagan asked, his face lighting up like a schoolboy's.

"We found some references to it," Doc said. "Diagrams, notes, equations. But none of it seemed valid. The other scientist and I dismissed most of it. I then went back to the European Theater, where we were reunited."

Deagan clucked his tongue and gave a short, quick shake of his head. "Yeah, them were the days, all right."

"Who was this other scientist?" Ace asked.

"A man named Walter Jennings. He still works for the government in the Bureau of Research and Development in Washington, D.C. I need you to contact him in person. See if he knows the whereabouts of the plans for Tesla's particle ray destabilizer."

"When?" Deagan asked.

"This afternoon, if possible," Doc said. "I've taken the liberty of calling the airport. They're readying one of our planes for the flight. That is, if you're available to be the pilot."

Ace grinned. "Consider me ready."

"Just make sure there's a parachute on board for me," Deagan said, his grin almost as wide as Ace's.

Before anyone could speak, the telephone on the desk rang. Doc ignored it, as was his custom, as did Ace, but Deagan jumped out of his chair and grabbed it.

"Yeah?" He listened intently, then looked at Doc and covered the mouthpiece. "It's O'Bannion, the doorman. Says there's a reporter downstairs from the Post wanting to see you. Has a box of stuff."

"I've been expecting that," Doc said. "Send the elevator down for him."

Deagan spoke into the phone again, then smirked. As he hung up he looked at Doc again. "O'Bannion says it ain't a he, it's a she. And a looker at that."

Ace's brow wrinkled. "Did she give a name?"

"I didn't ask," Deagan said, cocking his head. "Why?"

"Never mind," Ace said, using the cane to boost himself out of the chair. He had once moved with the nimbleness of an Olympic fencer until a burst of German shrapnel had torn through his leg at the close of the war. He'd still managed to fly double the number of missions both as a fighter and bombardier pilot in the skies over Germany. "I need to check the monitor."

As he hurried from the library, Deagan and Doc exchanged glances, then Deagan grinned. "I got a hunch what this little vignette is all about. Excuse me." He rose from his chair and hurried after Assante, easily catching him in the hallway.

"What's your hurry?" Deagan asked, clamping his huge left hand on Ace's shoulder.

"No hurry. I just need to check something, that's all."

The grin never left Deagan's face. He matched Ace step-for-step as they went to view the television monitor. An extremely pretty, dark haired woman in her early twenties stood looking up at the camera. Her arms framed her breasts as she carried a large valise in front of her using both hands.

Deagan raised his eyebrows. "Wow, O'Bannion called this one, all right. She is a looker. And then some."

Ace had a look of burgeoning panic on his face. He glanced back toward the library, and then to Deagan.

"Tom, I need you to do something for me."

"Oh, it's *Tom* now?" Deagan said. "Not Mad Dog or 'hey, you?'"

Ace glanced at the elevator and then back to Deagan, flashing a nervous smile. "That girl…"

"Yeah, I'm looking forward to meeting her." Deagan glanced at the monitor again. "I wonder what her name is?"

Ace compressed his lips. "Her name is Penelope Cartier. I know her."

"Yeah, that's right." Deagan snapped his fingers. "You and her were mentioned in the society page a couple a weeks ago, weren't yah? Something about a hot romance?"

"Hardly the word for it," Ace said. "Look, do me a favor and tell her I'm not here if she asks."

"Why don't you tell her yourself?"

Ace frowned, shook his head, and glanced back at the elevator doors. "Look, Tom, just do this for me, okay? I'll be in the library."

"The library?" The grin on Deagan's face took on a lascivious aspect. "Don't tell me you're afraid she's gonna say the rabbit died, or something."

Ace's head shook in frustration and he started a quick trek down the hallway. "Remember what I said. I'm not here."

Deagan laughed at his friend's hasty retreat as he walked over to the elevator. The doors opened and the stunningly beautiful woman stepped out, carrying the valise with both hands and flashing a smile that Deagan thought would light up half of Times Square. She extended her hand.

"You must be Colonel Deagan," she said. "I'm Penelope Cartier, from the *New York Daily News*. Penny, for short. I'm here to see Doc Atlas."

Deagan immediately reached down and grabbed the valise. He hefted it quite easily, but raised he eyebrows. "Say, this is kinda' heavy. You shoulda' told O'Bannion to have me come down to lug it up here for yah."

"You're such a gentleman," she said, brushing back some of her dark hair. "That's so refreshing these days."

"CAR-TEE-EH." Deagan smiled and directed her toward Doc's office. "That a French name?"

"American." Penny laughed.

Deagan's grin widened. After knocking on the door, and getting a command to enter, he opened it and they saw Doc Atlas standing by his desk. Penelope Cartier's eyes widened.

"Doc, this is Penny," Deagan said. "She brought over this stuff for you."

Doc nodded and said, "Thank you, Miss, for your promptness." He started to turn away.

"My promptness?" she said. "Is that all the thanks I get for lugging that heavy case all the way across town on the bus? Which I had to pay for out of my own pocket, I might add."

Doc regarded her for a moment. "Thomas, please escort this young lady down to secretarial and get a voucher for a taxi fare back to her newspaper office."

"I'd be more interested in hearing about why you're so interested in what our morgue had on Nikola Tesla," Penny said. "And if it has anything to do with this latest extortion scheme involving the Dark Destroyer."

"Regrettably, I'm afraid we have some pending appointments," Doc said. "Perhaps another time."

"Another time?" She flashed another high-wattage smile. "If you could just give me a little bit of info..."

Doc said nothing.

"Come on," she said. "I've spent the last four years writing all sorts of front page articles while all you guys were away overseas, and now that you're all back, I'm reduced to being a stringer again. I need a story with some beef to get back into the big boy's league."

Doc's face showed no emotion. "As I said, thank you for your prompt and assiduous assistance, Miss." Doc said. "I'll have my secretarial staff duplicate the contents of the articles and have them sent by messenger back to you." He paused as his eyes swept over her. "What did you say you're name was?"

"Penelope Cartier," she said, flashing another high-wattage smile. "But you can call me Penny."

"I'll watch for your byline," Doc said. "I'm sure with your determination, it will come soon enough. Thomas will show you out, Miss Cartier."

"Don't I even get a hint about what this story might be about?" The smile waned a bit in the face of Doc's non-response. "Does Tesla's research fit in with that explosion last night on the waterfront? Is that death ray thing for real?"

Again, Doc said nothing.

Deagan gently touched her arm, urging the protesting woman toward the door. In the hallway, he said, "Don't feel bad, Penny. Doc sort of marches to the beat of his own drummer."

"You can say that again." Her tone was frosty. "Say, have you seen Ace Assante around here this morning?"

Deagan's mouth tugged at the corners, but he shrugged and shook his head. "Can't say where he is right now."

"Figures." She opened her purse and took out a pack of cigarettes. "Got a light?"

He held up his hands. "Don't take it personal, or nothing, but Doc don't like nobody smoking around him."

"Around him? He's in the other room." She put the cigarette between her lips.

Deagan reached into his pocket and removed his lighter, but didn't flip it open. "I'll light it as soon as we're down in secretarial, okay? I'm in enough trouble already."

She frowned and put the cigarette back into the pack. "I'm trying to cut down anyway. Let's go get that damn voucher."

• • •

"Don't take it personal, or nothing, but Doc don't like nobody smoking around him."

Penny stood in the shade of the Empire State Building and lighted her smoke. She was in the corner and had a bird's eye view of the Fifth Avenue side of the building. She figured Doc Atlas and his crew would most likely leave by that exit, since that was closest to the ground floor doors of his private elevator. She wondered what kind of influence this Atlas guy had to merit a private elevator and two floors in the tallest building in the world. She knew he was a war hero, a scientist, and inventor. Plus, he was obviously rich. The morgue had a few articles about him on file, mostly centering on his rich philanthropist father. There were a couple pictures of him being out socially with some pretty daughter of an anthropologist. The pictures hadn't done him justice, though. In person his physical presence was … well, a bit breathtaking.

Easy, girl, she thought as she drew in some smoke. It tasted hot and bitter.

No wonder that Atlas guy doesn't like people to smoke around him, she thought. *I don't even like it myself, sometimes.*

Two men leaving the building caught her eye and she immediately lifted the newspaper she'd been carrying for cover. As she carefully peeked over the top edge, she saw the two were Assante and Deagan. So much for Ace not being there, the cad. And for Deagan, too, lying to cover for his buddy. Just like a man. But why was Ace avoiding her? She considered this and figured that a guy like him, with his choice of women, probably wouldn't want to get tied down to one set of legs.

She smirked.

And neither do I, she thought.

The two of them were so busily engaged in what appeared to be an ongoing argument they didn't even notice her. Deagan hailed a cab and Penny worked her way toward the edge of the sidewalk, still holding the newspaper in front of her.

They got in and the hack took off from the curb.

A man was opening the rear door of another nearby taxi. Penny stepped over to the open door and held her stomach.

"Do you mind, sir?" she said. "I've got to get to the hospital. My sister's about to have a baby."

The man's jaw dropped and he stepped back.

Penny got inside and leaned toward the driver. "See that cab that just took off?"

The driver grunted.

"Follow it," she said. "And there's an extra tip in it for you if can keep it low ball."

The driver grunted again and shifted into first.

Penny checked her purse. She had barely enough for cab fare, but she did have that voucher that the head secretary had given her.

Pretty girl, she thought. *If you like the Maureen O'Hara type.* And Deagan obviously was enamored with her. Not that she'd shown any sign of returning the attraction. In fact, the secretary had been downright frosty toward the big ox.

Ahead, the cab with Deagan and Assante weaved in and out of traffic.

"Don't lose them," Penny said.

"Relax," the cab driver said. "I know where they're going. I heard the driver radio it in. There's a private airport on the outskirts of the city."

Penny rechecked her purse. "Like I said, you get me there without them seeing us and there'll be a fin in it for you."

"Piece of cake."

A private airport, Penny thought. Looks like the chase ends there. *Unless…*

She fingered the voucher that Polly St. Claire had given her and smiled. Maybe not.

• • •

Deagan silently chuckled, feigning ignorance as Ace craned his neck to look out the rear window of the taxi.

"You're sure that was she?" Ace said, the space between his eyebrows furrowing. "Back on Fifth Avenue?"

"*She*?" Deagan laughed.

Ace frowned. "Oh, I forgot that proper grammar is the last thing you'd understand. *Was it her?*"

"Yep," Deagan said. "She had a paper in front of her face, but you can't hide gams like she's got." He paused and rubbed his chin with a pair of fingers the size of sausages. "I gotta say, you're one lucky man."

Ace turned back and frowned. "Will you lay off?"

Deagan shrugged. "Well, I ain't insinuating nothing, you understand."

"You'd better not."

Deagan canted his head and feigned a contemplative look. "She couldn't be very far along, could she? I mean, you two haven't been going out that long, have yah?"

"I thought I told you to knock it off?"

"So?" Deagan said. "Did yah?"

Ace rolled his eyes. "For a supposed officer and gentleman, you have a distinct absence of couth."

"I'm just trying to do the math, is all." Deagan began ticking off his fingers, like he was silently counting. "I coulda' swore I heard her asking Polly if she could recommend a good attorney. One that specializes in paternity cases."

The blood seemed to drain from Assante's face.

• • •

Doc Atlas shone the powerful underwater search light over the collected debris on the floor of the harbor. The depth wasn't excessive at this juncture, perhaps only sixty feet or so, but the detritus of a near constant flow of bilge and rubbish both from sea vessels and on shore dumping made the search for any traces of the recently destroyed boat very problematic. Although he'd been able to estimate the location of the sunken pleasure craft from the previous night's explosion, the lack of a precisely marked location and the omnipresent currents had made the search of the area more difficult. Doc had elected to rent traditional, hardhat diving gear rather than trying to use a SCUBA device. Diving alone in the murkiness of the channel was precarious enough, and with the tether line he at least felt a modicum of security. If Deagan and Ace had been available to accompany him on this dive, it would have afforded more possibilities.

The beam of the search light swept over a misshapen block of metal perhaps three feet by five feet in diameter. Doc pinpointed the location. It appeared to be a large section of a motor, the same kind the sunken pleasure craft might have had. He tugged at the tether line, giving himself more slack, and proceeded to march toward the wreckage. In his other hand he held the steel cable with which he could secure any item of interest to have it winched to the surface.

He stopped at the twisted hunk and scrutinized it. It was definitely a motor of some sort. Moving the light in an ever-widening circle, he surveyed the area nearby. His heavy steps had stirred wafting layers of silt from the harbor bottom and as he waited for them to undulate away, he felt a definitive double tug on his tether line, accompanied by a transmission from the boat to helmet telephone.

"Doctor Atlas, sir. It's Captain Roddy. The Coast Guard's here requesting you surface."

Doc leaned back slightly and peered through the circular faceplate of his helmet. Two pointed, rectangular shapes floated side-by-side about sixty feet above him. Another boat had joined the craft he'd rented. Bending forward quickly, Doc looped the cable around the damaged, misshapen motor and secured it. He then retraced his steps back so he could begin his assent to the boat above.

"Very well," Doc said. "I'm ready. I've secured an item for you to winch up, once I surface."

For a few seconds there was no reply, and then Roddy's voice came back on the line.

"Errr, they're advising a negative on the removal of anything from the bottom, sir."

This puzzled Doc, but he replied in the affirmative. However, he did not unsecure the cable from the remnants of the damaged motor.

"I'm ready to surface," Doc said. "Bring me up."

Doc felt another double tug of the line, signaling that they would be pulling him to the surface. Suddenly, the steel cable alongside him pulled taut and the motor he'd secured began a rapid ascent. The winch was being retraced at a faster rate than Doc's assent. He tried to glance downward to gauge the progress of the motor, but the helmet and the angle of his ascent blocked his line of vision.

The retracting cable drew close to him and continued to move upward. Suddenly Doc felt something collide with his heavy, metal boots. His ascent doubled in speed, and he realized he was being pulled upward by the winch, which was being retracted at a far greater rate of speed than a safe ascent permitted. Surfacing too fast would surely result in nitrogen narcosis, which meant he would need to immediately get to a decompression chamber, and the whereabouts of one would be dubious. He tried to kick his heavy boots loose from the motor but they had become entangled in the metallic shroud. The tension on the line was so great that he couldn't disengage the catch to free the snared motor.

"Stop the winch," Doc said. "I'm snagged on the cable."

No reply. His assent did not slow.

"Do you read me?" Doc said again.

Still no reply.

He estimated that he was now approximately forty feet from the surface. Reaching down, he tried to pull his boots free. The assent was still proceeding at a bends-inducing rate. Doc reached for his diving knife and pulled it from its sheath. Fitting the blade against the leather straps securing the boots, he slashed the straps and felt the boots disengage. Using his legs to shove his body away, he watched through the port hole as the motor zoomed past him. Doc felt a sudden surge of cold wetness as the water began winding its way up the legs of the canvas diving suit, capturing the air inside and causing the rest of the suit to bulge outward against the trapped air. He immediately released the weighted belt from around his waist. The new found buoyancy would cause him to get to the surface at too fast a rate as well. Sheathing the knife, Doc used both his hands to grip the helmet and gave it a hard twist to the right. The pressure was too great and prevented the helmet from disengaging from the corselet. Estimating he was still about thirty-five feet below the surface, Doc felt the numbness spreading through his body from the cold water that continued to penetrate the damaged suit.

Unsheathing the knife once more, he took a deep breath of the remaining air and reached upward, slashing the life line and then he oxygen hose. He immediately ceased his upward movement. Doc let the knife drop from his fingers and once again gripped the helmet and gave it a mighty twist. This time it moved, rotating away from the corselet and sinking away from him in the dark water. Still impeded by the heavy suit and the remaining metal of the corselet, Doc began kicking his powerful legs and paddling with his arms. The surface lingered many feet above him like the lid of a liquid coffin.

The distance to be traveled looked to be insurmountable, but Doc fought against the incipient panic. The blood felt like it was banging against his internal vessels and his tortured lungs screamed for oxygen. He still had at least twenty feet or more to go. The lid of the liquid coffin appeared brighter, but a sudden impingement occurred as black dots begin to swarm into his vision. His powerful limbs continued to propel him upward, toward the surface.

Fifteen feet… Twelve… Ten…

The black dots coalesced, blocking out everything but a pinpoint of light.

His head broke free of the surface and the air caressed his face like a grateful lover's touch, snapping him back to consciousness. Doc began treading water, taking in great breaths as he fixed his position in relation to the boats. They were perhaps fifteen yards away. Several men raced nervously back and forth, scanning the surface of the water as they fished out the severed air hose and lifeline. One of them turned, spotted Doc and began yelling.

Roddy ran to the side of the boat, grinned, and removed a life preserver from the side wall of the cabin. He hurled it toward Doc and it skipped over the water. Doc swam toward it, feeling his breathing and his strained limbs returning to a semblance of normalcy. He gripped the circular life preserver and straightened his body out as he was pulled in by Roddy and one of his crew. Four other men, two in Coast Guard uniforms and two in suits, stood on the deck and watched. One of them Doc recognized: Arthur Smith. The other's identity was unknown.

When Doc was alongside the boat Roddy extended his arm and helped Doc aboard.

"Thank God you're all right," Roddy said. "What happened down there?"

"I became entangled in that recovered motor." Doc indicated the damaged suit. "I had to disengage or risk becoming afflicted with decompression sickness."

Roddy flashed a gap-toothed smile. "Not many men could've done what you did."

"Was the recovered item brought on board?" Doc asked.

"I'm afraid that's being confiscated," Smith said, stepping forward. His face looked a bit pastier than it had earlier.

Doc regarded the man with a sharp look.

"This is part of an ongoing, government investigation," Smith continued. "One that you stepped into without authorization."

"I intended to examine that wreckage," Doc said. "I believe it quite possibly was part of that boat that was blown up last night."

On the other side of the boat the winch swung outward, lowering the recovered motor to the deck of the Coast Guard boat.

Smith cocked a thumb toward the other craft. "We'll do the examination, Atlas."

"I fully intended to share my findings with you, Agent Smith," Doc said.

Smith's lips twisted into something akin to a smile. "Like I said, we'll do the examination ourselves. Despite your interest, and now your involvement in all this, you're nothing but a private citizen."

"Doctor Atlas," Captain Roddy said. "This joker and his partner stepped in and hit the retraction switch on the cable as we was pulling you up. I yelled at them to shut it down, but they must've jammed it or something. Couldn't shut it off and we was busy trying to pull you up safely." The captain turned to Smith with a scowl. "You jerks could've killed this man with your carelessness. You know that?"

Smith eyed the other man for several seconds, then looked at Doc. "Good thing you're such a great swimmer."

Doc said nothing.

Smith licked his lips, turned and watched as the Coast Guard crew removed the cable and secured the recovered motor. "Looks like we're all set. See yah around, Atlas. Next time don't forget your swim fins."

Doc still said nothing.

Roddy lurched forward, his fist balled up, but Smith pivoted and delivered a quick, overhand right that knocked the charging captain into oblivion.

Doc moved forward and caught the falling man.

Smith back peddled and removed a Government Model Colt .45 from a shoulder holster. The other members of the crew immediately stopped.

"I hardly think that's necessary," Doc said, lowering Roddy to the deck and then kneeling to check the man's vitals.

The other man in the suit smirked. The two Coast Guard officers looked a bit confused and shocked.

Smith held the .45 down by his leg, his eyes still centered on Doc. "Yeah, well, like I told yah, this is government business, so back off." He motioned everyone toward the Coast Guard boat, but turned before stepping on the parallel deck.

"See you around, Atlas."

"Undoubtedly, you shall," Doc replied.

• • •

Washington D.C.

Mad Dog Deagan continued to pace up and down in the rather small waiting room of the Bureau of Research and Development on Avenue J of the nation's capitol. Assante sat in a nearby chair and lighted his fourth cigarette, an amused smile on his handsome face. His ebony cane with the ornate handle was next to him.

"I know you spent a good deal of time in the infantry," Ace said. "But all that marching back and forth you're doing is going to wear a hole in the carpet."

Deagan frowned. "Yeah, well, it'll serve them right. They got no business making us wait so damn long. Don't they know who we are?"

Assante blew a cloud of smoke toward the ceiling. "It seems they don't care."

Deagan's lips curled from a frown to a malevolent scowl. He strode to the secretary sitting at the desk next to the door separating them from the interior offices.

"How much longer we gonna have to wait?" he asked.

The girl leaned back in her chair, a terrified look on her face.

Assante stood up and strolled over, placing a hand on Mad Dog's shoulder.

"Please excuse my burly friend's demeanor," Ace said. "He's only recently been released from a hospital specializing in extremely volatile patients who are prone to violent outbursts. If you would be so kind as to check and see how soon we'll be able to see Dr. Jennings?" He punctuated his sentence with a smile that seemed to do wonders at reestablishing the young woman's disposition.

She picked up the phone and dialed, speaking softly into the receiver. After listening intently, the corners of her mouth tugged downward slightly and she nodded, murmuring something into the phone again. She replaced it in its cradle and looked up at Ace.

"They say it shouldn't be much longer, sir."

"Thank you," Assante said. "And you can call me Ace."

A starry-eyed smile dotted her mouth, but quickly vanished as Deagan emitted a low growling noise.

"That ain't good enough," he said as he moved to the door and twisted the handle. Finding it locked, he slammed his big fist against the door several times causing the entire frame to shake. "Jennings, I know you're in there. Now open this door and get your butt out here before I come in and drag you out."

The secretary's face was frozen in a look of sheer terror. Assante stepped over and patted her shoulder gently. Bending next to her ear, he whispered, "Don't worry, my dear. His bark is worse than his bite."

The girl hardly looked reassured.

The door opened and a heavyset, gray haired man in a lab coat stood there. He sported a Van Dyke goatee and his face was pale looking. His eyes looked enlarged behind the lenses of tortoise shell glasses.

Deagan's face twisted into what appeared to be a malevolent grin. "Dr. Jennings, I presume?"

The man nodded with hesitation. "I should tell you that I have nothing to say to you." His voice sounded weak. "Now please, leave. Tell Mr. DeMarco that I need a little more time."

Assante raised an eyebrow. "DeMarco? Johnny DeMarco?"

Jennings stiffened. "Who are you?"

"Listen, bub," Deagan said, thrusting his face about an inch in front of the other man's. "We're here at the request of Doc Atlas... I'm sure you heard of him. We got a few questions to ask you about your examination of Nikola Tesla's death ray plans."

Jennings licked his lips, his body trembling. "I...I have nothing to say." He looked toward the secretary. "Mary, call the authorities."

The girl immediately picked up the phone, but Assante leaned forward and hung it up, smiling all the while and shaking his head. He turned to the scientist. "Dr. Jennings, we only have a few quick questions for you, sir. We mean you no harm."

Jennings moved farther back, raising his arms in front of him in a defensive gesture. "Stay away from me. You're not who I thought you were, but I still don't want to talk to you."

Deagan's hand shot out and grabbed Jennings' arm. "You ain't going nowhere until you give us some answers."

A door opened behind them, and a voice said, "Let him go."

Deagan and Assante turned and saw three men standing in the doorway. One of them, a small man with the feral grin of a weasel, pointed a big, semi-automatic pistol at them. "You got a hearing problem, ape-man?"

Deagan's lower lip jutted out at the insult, but his fingers let go of Jennings lab coat.

"I never argue with a man holding a gun," Deagan said.

"Who are you gentlemen?" Assante asked.

"Federal agents," the little man said, the smile never leaving his face.

"Hey, I seen you before." Deagan pointed at the smaller, weasel-faced fellow. "You were at Doc's headquarters earlier today."

The little weasel smiled. "For a human gorilla, you got a good memory."

Deagan's face darkened with rage and he lurched forward, reaching for the smaller man. Ace grabbed him, but one of the other men clipped Deagan with a blackjack. The first blow stunned him and the man cocked his arm to deliver another. Ace stepped back as he twisted the handle of his cane, withdrawing a long blade from its wooden sheath. He thrust the blade into the man's shoulder, causing him to reel backward in pain.

"I wouldn't do that if I were you," Ace said.

"Can it, Assante," the weasel-faced man said. His face had a wide grin stretched over it, as he held a big, blue steel Colt .45 in his right hand. With the nimbleness of Fred Astaire, he danced back out of the range of the blade.

A stream of blood wound its way down Deagan's forehead from his thick crop of red hair. "If you think that'll stop me from getting to you, buster, you got another think coming."

The weasel's grin widened. "Even you can't stop a forty-five slug to the forehead, monkey man. Now both of yah, put up yer hands. You're under arrest."

"For what?" Deagan said.

"Yes," Ace said. "I'd like to be advised of the charges."

"You will be." The weasel jerked his hand toward the door. "Let's go. And hand over that pig sticker first."

Assante shook his head. "I took some shrapnel in my leg during the War. I need the cane for support."

The weasel aimed the pistol at Ace. "You can keep the cane, buster, but hand over the blade."

Assante considered the request, smiled, and handed the sword portion to one of the heavies.

As they pushed through the doors and into the late afternoon sunshine, Deagan saw a police car and paddy wagon pulling up the curb. Two uniformed D.C. coppers got out and approached them.

"What's going on here?" the coppers asked.

"Federal Agent Pauls," the weasel said, holding up a badge case. "Take these two in for A and B to a federal officer."

The copper's face twisted into a severe frown as he looked over Deagan and Assante. "The big one looks like he got what was coming to him already."

Deagan grinned. "If that little twerp hadn't been holding a gun on me, I'da shoved that sap where the sun don't shine."

"Tom, let me handle this." Ace turned to the cop. "Listen here, officer, I'm an attorney and I want to tell you that these spurious allegations are blatantly false, bordering on the preposterous, and if you take any actions against us, you'll be opening yourself up to a charge of false arrest."

"Yeah?" the copper said, a smile on his face. "You sound like a lawyer, all right." His mouth tightened back into a frown. "Flaherty, get over here and put the bracelets on these two and put 'em in the wagon."

"You're going to regret this," Assante said.

"Shaddup and turn around," the copper said. "You're under arrest."

"You're making a big mistake, buster," Deagan bellowed. "That guy Jennings is hiding something, and if that death ray thing is used again, it'll be on your heads."

• • •

Penny watched as Assante and Deagan were placed into the paddy wagon.

Serves them right, she thought. Especially that Ace. *Who did he think he was, hiding from me back in New York? Just wait till he calls again.*

But the words Deagan had yelled resonated within her: *The death ray*. So this was about that yacht exploding in New York last night. She considered the ramifications and quickly recalled the clippings from the morgue that she'd read on the way to Doc Atlas's headquarters.

Jennings...Deagan had also mentioned him. Penny knew that Atlas had been something of a modern marvel in both medicine and scientific research before enlisting in the Army once the war had started. She also remembered a clipping that he'd been back in New York on "leave" in '43, although it was widely speculated that the real reason was the government wanted him to help another scientist review some papers recovered from Nikola Tesla's apartment. One of them was purported to be the plans for some kind of particle beam, aka "the Death Ray." And Penny was certain that the name of the assisting scientist was Jennings. Dr. Walter Jennings.

The paddy wagon pulled away from the curb and the three men in suits watched its departure and then turned and hurried to a black Packard that was parked by the curb. The vehicle shot into traffic.

Penny wished she had enough money to hail a cab, but she was down to four nickels, three dimes, and two quarters. Luckily, she'd been able to modify the voucher that Atlas's secretary had given her for the cab ride into a free airplane ride following Deagan and Assante down here to the Capitol. It had worked out perfectly as her flight landed just as Ace and Deagan were strolling through the main foyer of the airport. Apparently flying your own airplane was convenient, but as Ace had mentioned on one of their dates, also a bit time consuming. Bribing the taxi driver to follow them once again as they departed had taken the rest of what little cash she'd had in her purse. Now she was wondering how she would be able to get back to New York, since the trail had virtually disappeared and the voucher was gone. Unless she wanted to go visit the two musketeers in the jail.

She smiled at the thought. It might almost be worth it to see the expression on Ace's face.

Instead, she walked over to a telephone booth and dialed the Operator. After placing a collect call to her editor, Jerry Martin, she waited, listening to her boss's surprised voice as the operator asked if he'd accept the charges. Penny was relieved when she heard him say, "Yes."

"Hi, Jerry," she said. "Thanks for taking my call."

The three men in suits watched the paddy wagon's departure...

"Penny?" His tone was a mixture of irritation and credulity. "Where the heck are you?"

"I'm in Washington. It's a long story, but, believe me, a big one. Remember that explosion near the harbor last night? The death ray tie-in?"

"Yeah." His voice sounded dubious.

"Well, I'm hot on the trail of what could blow the whole thing wide open. I followed two of Doc Atlas's boys to see a scientist that's mixed up in this."

"Mixed up how?"

"Not sure yet, but it's got to be big." She paused to let the potential for a dynamic headline form in his head. "We could scoop all the other papers in town. Heck, in the country. This is dynamite." She could hear his breathing and she knew she had him.

"Tell me more," he said.

"I wish I could, but I'm trying to follow someone. I've got to see a scientist named Walter Jennings. He's mixed up in this thing, and Atlas and he were involved in researching that death ray that Nikola Tesla came up with." She knew she was stretching things a little, but she had to bait the hook well. "I'm going to need you to wire me some money, as soon as possible."

Martin's sonorous breathing continued for a few seconds, then he spoke: "Okay, will do. Get to the nearest Western Union office and call me back."

"Swell, Jerry. Thanks." Penny looked up and saw a frumpy, middle-aged man with tortoise shell glasses and a van dyke beard waddling quickly out of the front doors of the building. He glanced around warily. She knew it was Jennings from the picture she'd seen in the news clipping of him and Atlas. For a moment she reflected on how stunningly handsome that Doc Atlas was, but quickly shifted that thought out of her head. She was on a story—A big story—one that could elevate her back to full-fledged news reporter status instead of the Girl Friday position to which she'd fallen now that all the men had returned from the War. "Jerry, I gotta go. Call you back later."

She heard a quip of protest on the phone, but hung up anyway. Jennings was almost at the main sidewalk now and she knew she couldn't afford to let this lead get away. Exiting the phone booth, Penny brushed back her thick expanse of dark hair and affected her most stunningly sincere and attractive smile.

"Professor Jennings," she said. "How nice to see you again."

Jennings stopped, his eyes widening behind the think lenses. "What? Who are you?"

"Penelope Cartier, *New York Daily News.*" She paused to assess the man.

His face was as white as a clip-on collar. "I need to ask you a few questions."

"Questions?" His brow furrowed. "About what?"

"About Tesla's particle beam."

"What." Jennings' face tightened. "I know nothing about that."

"You and Doc Atlas examined Tesla's papers back in forty-three, didn't you?"

Jennings shook his head, his mouth drawing down at the corners. "No. I don't know what you're talking about."

"You no doubt heard there was an explosion in New York City last nigh Do you think the beam was responsible?"

"Get away from me," Jennings said. "I told you—"

Penny suddenly felt someone grab her arms. She turned and saw the three men she'd seen with Deagan and Ace, the ones who'd ostensibly left in the black Packard. The big one held her fast. A smaller, unctuous looking man with a face resembling a rodent stepped up and displayed a pistol before sticking it back into his pocket.

"Let me go, you big creep," Penny said, her words laced with pain as the man squeezed her arms.

"Shaddup," the rodent-faced man said. "Try to scream and I'll ventilate you." He turned to Jennings. "Hiya, professor. Ain't seen you on the Lucky Lady lately."

Jennings looked completely ashen. His mouth drooped open but no words came out.

"Come on," the smaller man said, motioning toward the car. "We're all going for a ride."

• • •

Ace sat in silent frustration inside the twelve by twelve holding cell, staring at the flickering ceiling light in the hallway beyond the bars. He and the concrete slab he sat on had become well acquainted since they'd confiscated his cane. Deagan, on the other hand, paced like a caged beast.

"We've been locked up down here for over three hours," he bellowed for the twentieth time. "What the hell's going on here?"

Assante shook his head. When they were first incarcerated, he'd repeatedly requested to call another attorney to represent them, after informing them that neither one of them would answer any questions. Even after identifying himself as one of New York's most prominent trial lawyers and a partner in his father's prestigious law firm, the reaction was the same: silence.

Deagan grabbed the bars and shook them with all of his might, resembling a gorilla in a Republic jungle serial.

"When I get outta here, there's gonna be hell to pay." The veins bulged in Deagan's thick neck. "I'm gonna lay out every one of 'em."

"Will you sit down and shut up?" Ace said. "You're giving me a headache."

"So ask 'em for a Bromo, why don't yah." Deagan spun around. "Listen, ambulance chaser, you're the over-priced, high-society mouthpiece, do something. You gotta know every judge in New York City. One of them's gotta know somebody here in D.C. that can get us sprung."

"There's not much I can do if I can't contact anyone."

Deagan blew out an exasperated breath "Don't they know who I am?"

"Frankly, I don't think they really care," Ace said.

Mad Dog turned and grabbed the bars again. "Guard. Guard. I want to talk to someone right now." His words echoed down the deserted hallway.

"Keep making that racket," Ace grinned, "They'll think it's feeding time at the zoo."

Deagan turned to reply, but they both heard a door opening at the end of the hallway.

"About damn time," Deagan shouted. "You yellow bellied sons of—"

"Hey, Mad Dog," came the sonorous greeting. "Put a lid on it."

A wide grin spread across Deagan's broad face. "Koss. John Koss, you old salty SOB. What the hell you doing here?"

Two men stopped on the other side of the bars. One was a guard, and the other a distinguished, gray haired man in full dress Naval uniform. Admiral stars decorated the epaulets on his shoulders. "Hell, I should be asking you that question." He smiled and thrust his hand through the bars. "Been a few years, hasn't it?"

Ace coughed. "Would you like to introduce me to your friend?"

"Oh, yeah," Mad Dog released his friend's hand, "Ace Assante, lawyer, meet Admiral John Koss. Him and me crossed paths a couple of times in the Philippines."

Ace nodded his head. "Admiral, might I inquire what brings you down here to our humble abode?"

"Open up this cell immediately," the Admiral said to the guard who had escorted him down the hall. "Then leave us alone for a few minutes." The agent couldn't open the cell door fast enough.

"What you doin' here, What's the Navy—"

Koss held his hand up in front of Deagan's face until the guard had left. "The cops waited an hour for the federal agents who arrested you to show up to sign complaints. They never did. Eventually, the geniuses up-stairs made some phone calls and got a hold of me. As soon as I heard it was you, I came right down."

"Thanks pal."

The Admiral shrugged. "Hell, I still owe you."

"I'd like the names of the federal agents who accosted us," Ace said.

"So would I," Koss said. "Nobody seems to know who they are, or where they went."

Ace considered this for a moment. "So, I take it, we're free to go? No charges?"

The Admiral nodded. "But first, I have something to tell you both. And you can relay it to Doc Atlas when you see him. Back off your involvement in this Death Ray matter. There are classified avenues being pursued. We can handle it from here. It's a military issue. Just drop it, okay?"

"Admiral," Ace said, "first a boat blows up in the harbor after an extor-tion threat, then we're stone-walled by the scientist who reviewed Tesla's research with Doc Atlas and thrown into jail by some mysterious govern-ment agents and kept incommunicado. Now, a high ranking naval officer, obviously a well-respected war hero, shows up and orders us to stop our pursuit of what could be a weapon of great destruction that could be un-leashed on New York City." He raised an eyebrow. "What do you think of that, Mad Dog?"

"It's nuts," Deagan said. "Hey, we're the good guys here, John. What's so secret that Doc Atlas and his most trusted companions can't be let in on?" He paused. "Wait a minute, I remember Doc saying all of Tesla's papers were turned over to the Department of the Navy… What are you hiding?"

The Admiral's mouth compressed into a thin line. "There's a lot more at stake here than appears on the surface. Now just do what I said and drop your inquiries."

Deagan and Ace exchanged glances. Deagan's eyes narrowed and he nodded at Ace.

"Thank you for your advice and concern, Admiral," Assante said. "But since both former Colonel Deagan and I are private citizens and no longer in the military, I you won't be too offended if we ignore your suggestion."

"Yeah, that goes double for me, too." Deagan brushed past the Admiral as he left the cell. "Come on, shyster, we got work to do."

• • •

Manhattan, New York City

Doc Atlas glanced again at the rearview mirror from the back seat of the taxi as they moved through the substantial traffic on Sixth Avenue and mentally reviewed his afternoon spent at the New York City Morgue. At the mayor's request, the city coroner, Doctor Rosenblatt, had called Doc in to assist with the autopsies of the two bodies that had been pulled from the Hudson River. If there were any other persons aboard the yacht that exploded the previous night, their remains were lost to the thick, muddy waters that flowed to the ocean. Both bodies were male, determined to be between thirty and forty years of age, and badly charred. Rosenblatt had worked with Doc Atlas several times before the War, and welcomed Doc's assistance in this high profile "Death Ray" case.

Doc was certain of one thing: neither man had been alive prior to the explosion on the yacht.

He looked at the rearview mirror once again and locked eyes with the taxicab driver.

"You're Doc Atlas, ain't yah?" the man said.

Doc replied with a fractional nod.

"Thought so," the driver said. "I remember seeing your picture in the papers back when you was home on leave and busted up that Nazi spy ring here in the city."

Doc recalled the incident and let the trace of a smile adorn his lips.

"Yeah, that was something, all right," the driver continued. He stopped talking and swore at another car that cut in front of them. After expelling an exasperated breath, he glanced back at Doc. "Sorry, Dr. Atlas. New York City's got to have the worst drivers in the whole blamed nation."

Doc said nothing.

"Anyway," the hack driver said. "You're a real hero in my book. I heard what you did in the War, going on all them commando missions, and then helping out to treat the wounded after D-Day."

"I merely did what I could to assist."

The driver pursed his lips. "My son lost a leg in the Battle of the Bulge."

"I'm sorry to hear that," Doc said.

As they waited at the traffic light to turn onto Fifth Avenue, Doc once again glanced at the rear view mirror.

"Has that black Ford sedan been behind us since we left the morgue?" he asked.

The cab driver squinted into the mirror. "Say, you know, it has. I was gonna mention that to yah, too." He paused and licked his lips. "Want me to shake 'em?"

"Not at this time," Doc said. He turned back in an attempt to see the other vehicle's license plate, but there was none affixed to the bumper.

The light turned green and the hack driver moved out into the intersection, waiting to make the left turn. After waiting through the entire light cycle, he managed a turn on the yellow. The black sedan followed them leaving a spoor of burned rubber.

"They're still on our tail," the driver said.

Suddenly the cab lurched forward after a noisy collision to its rear end.

The taxi driver's body jerked, and he slowed and began rolling down his window as the black Ford pulled alongside.

"What's your problem, mack?" the taxi driver yelled. "You clipped the rear end of my hack."

The other driver, a swarthy looking guy with a thick mustache, grinned and shook his head. The passenger of the black sedan appeared to be a man of substantial girth. He rolled down the passenger side window. "Sorry," he said. Pointing to an upcoming alleyway. "Pull in there and we can check for any damage." He held up a five dollar bill.

"It'll take a lot more than that if this rig's scratched," the taxi driver said, maneuvering the steering wheel toward the mouth of the alley.

Doc leaned forward in the seat. "Listen to me very carefully. I believe that those men have nefarious intentions. Come to a stop and I'll get out. Then you immediately drive to the opposite end of the alley and wait."

"Huh? Wait for what?"

Doc didn't answer. Instead, he gripped the door handle as the taxi turned into the alley, the black sedan perhaps ten feet behind it.

They turned into the alley, the dark car following behind them. As the taxi came to a halt, Doc pushed open the door and stepped out, motioning for the taxi driver to leave. Malevolent grins twisted onto the faces of the two men in the sedan and both reached inside their jackets as the sedan sped forward. Doc took two steps and jumped on top of the hood, touching it lightly and then landing on the roof. A gunshot from within the vehicle sounded and a hole ripped through the metal next to his foot. Doc shifted his weight to maintain his balance and then dropped to the alley floor, landing like a big jungle cat. The sedan jerked to a stop and both doors opened. The driver pushed out the door, bringing up a large revolver, but Doc grabbed the man's wrist, pushing the barrel of the weapon away. It discharged into the rear fender. Doc twisted the gangster's body so that it was between him and the second gunman. The second gunman slammed his huge arms on top of the roof of the car, a big semi-auto in his large hands. The semi-auto bucked as it was fired and the bullet tore into the gunman Doc was holding. The man yelled in pain and tried to wiggle loose. Doc tore the revolver from the man's slack fingers with his right hand and lifted the man's body up and over the roof with his left. The big gangster on the other side of the car was struck by the flying leg of his partner. Doc ran around the rear of the sedan, righting the revolver in his hands as he ran.

Doc quickly sized up the man. He had to be about six foot six and built like an icebox. The brute brushed away his partner's body and again leveled the pistol at Doc, but the Golden Avenger grabbed the weapon and twisted it out of the other man's hands. He then smashed the long barrel of the revolver against the big man's temple. He sagged to his knees, then snapped back, charging like an enraged bull. Doc stepped nimbly aside and grabbed the gangster by his shoulders, flinging him into the side of the building. The large man's shoulder took the brunt of the crash, but he turned and smiled.

The distinctive click of a switchblade knife split the air. The big hoodlum began to advance with the knife held in front of him.

"I'm gonna cut you," he said.

Doc pointed the revolver at him and ordered the man to drop the knife.

The big hoodlum's smile twisted into a scowl and he continued forward, apparently unafraid of the gun.

"You ain't gonna shoot me," he muttered.

Doc considered this statement and realized that the man was an imminent threat. Still, taking him alive so that he could be interrogated was preferable. Doc took two steps back and fired a round into the big man's left knee. The man-mountain grunted in pain and fell forward, the blood coursing down his pant leg.

"Drop the knife," Doc repeated.

The big crook glanced up at him, malevolence in his eyes, and hurled the blade straight at Doc's body.

As he pivoted out of the path of the hurled knife, Doc's peripheral vision caught the furtive movement of his foe. The man had grabbed the pistol from the ground.

As the big gangster was bringing the weapon up to fire, Doc pointed the revolver and squeezed the trigger. The round caught his assailant in the forehead. After a quick, jerking motion of his head, the would-be killer crumpled forward.

Doc retrieved the .45 from the dead man's hand.

The cab driver appeared at Doc's side, out of breath from running.

"Man, that was something," the taxi driver said. "You all right?"

Doc nodded. In the distance, he could hear the wail of sirens.

• • •

Deserted Airstrip near Alexandria, Virginia

Penny could barely feel her hands. The cords securing her were so tight she was certain the circulation had been severely impaired. Her feet, which were similarly secured, ached, too. She attempted to roll onto her side in the dirty bed of the truck. The front of her dress had been ripped open, exposing her brassiere. After being abducted in front of the government research building, she and Jennings had been transferred from one vehicle to another, finally ending up in the dark interior of this truck with no light whatsoever. She heard the drone of an approaching motor, but it didn't sound like a car, or even another truck. More like an airplane.

Could that be right? There were no ambient sounds of civilization, other than the sputtering of the plane. It grew louder, like it was going to land. They must be at some sort of remote airstrip.

Jennings's voice startled her in the darkness. "It won't be long now, I'm afraid."

Penny was relatively shocked that the taciturn professor had spoken to her at all. He'd barely said three words since their capture.

"You know where we are?" she asked.

He didn't reply.

"Talk to me, damn you."

"I'm sorry for all of this, young lady." His voice wavered. "I wish you'd heeded my warning and left back there."

"Yeah?" She felt a twinge of pain as her bare arm rubbed against the coarse grain of the wooden floor. "Well, how about showing it and trying to untie my hands."

After a few moments of silence, Jennings replied. "I can't do that. I'm tied up, too."

Penny swore at the man. "At least you could *try*. What do you think these goons have in mind for us, anyway? Tea and crumpets?"

More silence, punctuated by a soft, hiccupping sound. Jennings was crying.

"Oh, brother," Penny said. "Of all the bad luck... I get kidnapped by gangsters along with Casper Milquetoast."

"You're not being fair," Jennings said. "And they're not gangsters."

"Well who are they, then?"

The sobbing continued.

"At least tell me what you know, dammit," she said.

"All right. I'll tell you." His voice cracked. When he spoke again, it was in a low whisper. "They work for the government..."

• • •

The Empire State Building

Deagan and Ace continued to argue as the elevator reached the 88th floor with its customary non-stop swiftness. As the doors opened they were surprised to see Doc Atlas standing in the hallway.

"There have been some new developments." Doc turned and strode toward the library. Deagan and Assante followed. They both sat in the fine, leather backed chairs as Doc stood by the front of the room.

"I assume from your earlier phone call, Thomas, that your trip to Washington was not a productive one," Doc said.

Deagan snorted. "You can say that again. I think there's more to this whole thing than meets the eye."

"You have a distinct talent for understating the obvious," Ace said.

"Listen, shyster, if you hadn't been there slowing me down, I'da dragged that Jennings character back here by the scruff of his neck to answer our questions."

Before Ace could continue with the repartee, Doc raised his palm.

"Professor Jennings is missing," he said. "As is that young lady from the newspaper who brought us the files this morning."

Ace hunched forward. "What? Penny's missing, too?"

Doc nodded. "Apparently Miss Cartier showed a bit of ingenuity with the travel voucher Polly gave her to cover the taxi ride. She apparently followed you to the airfield and found out you were taking our plane to D.C. Then she modified the voucher and used it to secure a flight there by herself."

Deagan frowned. "Some girlfriend you got there, Ace."

"I told you, she's *not* my girlfriend."

"Regardless," Doc said, his voice harboring a tinge of irritation. "She followed you down there and contacted her editor about doing a story about Dr. Jennings. He left the building soon after you two were taken into custody and has not been seen or heard from since. This all occurred over six hours ago."

Deagan's mouth twitched. "Man, I hope Penny's all right. I liked her pluck."

"She's a very nice girl," Ace added.

"The question remains," Doc said. "Whom did you say ordered your arrest in D.C.?"

"It was one of them guys that was here earlier," Deagan said. "The little one with the face like a rat."

"Good analogy," Ace said.

"Special Agent Dexter Pauls," Doc said. "I did some checking. Neither he, nor the man who identified himself as Agent Arthur Smith, is affiliated with the Federal Bureau of Investigation. Director Hoover is most upset that these two men had counterfeit identification."

"I knew that guy was a rat." Deagan fingered the lump on his head from the blackjack. "No wonder they never showed at the jailhouse to sign complaints. The whole thing was a ruse to get us out of the picture so they could grab Jennings."

"And Penny probably got in their way." Ace's mouth compressed into a thin line.

"Additionally," Doc said, "there was an attempt on my life while I was en route back here from the morgue."

"What?" Deagan lurched forward. "What happened?"

Doc shook his head fractionally. "Two men accosted me. Unfortunately, I had to tactically neutralize them before I could gather any intelligence from them. They were known to the police, however. Apparently, they were associates of Johnny DeMarco."

"DeMarco," Ace said. "Jennings mentioned his name when we tried to question him."

"Yeah," Deagan said. "Like he thought we were some of DeMarco's boys."

"As I'm sure you know," Doc said, "DeMarco owns a floating gambling ship that is nestled just outside the three mile limit of the coast."

"The Lucky Lady," Ace said.

Deagan gave him a sharp look.

Ace shrugged. "I've been there a few times."

"So, apparently, has Dr. Jennings," Doc said. "I recall that he's something of an inveterate gambler."

"So it's a good bet that Jennings and maybe Penny are on board that floating crap game." Deagan stood. "Maybe we'd better pay DeMarco a little visit."

"My sentiments exactly," Ace said.

"Given the attempt on my life earlier by men purported to be in De-Marco's employ," Doc said, "we shouldn't go there unarmed."

Ace shook his head. "That could be a problem. DeMarco's goons search everybody coming aboard the boat for weapons."

Doc reached onto a nearby chair and grabbed a mid-sized brown va-lise. "I assumed that might be the case, which is why I prepared this." He unzipped the case displaying a large amount of bundled currency, then patted the bottom. "There is a hollow compartment here that can house three pistols and several magazines."

Deagan grinned. "Ain't nothing that beats a good old forty-five."

Doc zipped up the valise, then fixed them both with a concerned look. "I'm not sure how all this is connected, but the Dark Destroyer has made another extortion demand, about an hour ago. This time raising the amount to seven-hundred-fifty thousand dollars, or he claims he'll destroy the Statue of Liberty or Coney Island."

Deagan whistled. "That's a lot of dough. What did they tell him?"

"I've convinced them to fictitiously agree to pay the money," Doc said.

Ace perked up. "What?"

Doc held up his hand again. "When they obtain the location of the drop-off of the ransom, we'll be the ones proceeding there. Hopefully, we can apprehend these villains before any more lives are lost."

"But what if they use that death ray thing again?" Deagan asked.

Doc stared at him, saying nothing.

• • •

New York Harbor

The late evening mist stung their faces as the ferry boat chugged up alongside the Lucky Lady. The ship was anchored just out of the legal range of the authorities, although it was known to periodically venture down the coast docking at such places as Atlantic City, Charlotte, Miami, and Havana. Its owner, Johnny DeMarco, also went by the nickname, Captain Lucky.

The rubber tires that lined the sides of the ferry bumped against the substantial steel of the ship. Crew members quickly gathered mooring lines as the elevator was lowered from the ship's deck.

Deagan, who had donned a pinstripe suit, a garish looking ascot, and a fedora leaned forward. "When they gonna do the search?"

"As soon as we get off the lift," Ace said. He was the only one of the three who had not changed clothes.

Doc, who was now wearing a large overcoat and a hat pulled down low on his forehead, adjusted the shoulder holster with the huge .45 Colt revolver.

The elevator arrived and people began lining up to get on board. Doc and company were on the last trip. As the lift stopped at the top, a trio of hoodlums opened the iron gate that had secured the riders and motioned for everyone to step off. A pair of stocky women, who could've doubled for female wrestlers, stood nearby casually smoking.

"No guns or knives allowed on board," one of the hoods announced. "Ladies, open your purses and step over there to be checked by Olga and Katrina. Gents, form up over here."

"You gonna do a short-arm inspection?" asked Deagan. It had been previously decided that Mad Dog was going to play the part of a rich gambler and friend of Ace's, while the disguised Doc Atlas would masquerade as the gambler's bodyguard.

The hood looked perplexed. "Short-arm inspection? What you talking about?"

Deagan laughed. "Guess you missed out on the War, eh, sonny? What were you, four-F?"

The hoodlum frowned and reached for Deagan.

Doc's hand shot out and grabbed the hood's arm, causing him to sink to his knees. The two other hoods drew pistols.

"Gentlemen, gentlemen," Assante said, stepping forward. "Please watch where you place your hands. This is Mr. Roscoe T. Markham, oil tycoon out of Texas, and his bodyguard, Goliath."

"Tell the big lug to let Marty go," one of the hoods said.

Ace turned and made a dismissive gesture toward Doc, who released the hoodlum.

"And tell him to hand over that gat he's carrying in his shoulder rig," the other hood said.

Again, Ace motioned toward Doc, who unsnapped the gun and held it with some hesitation.

"Take it easy, Gargantuan," the hood said, hooking his thumb toward a

"When they gonna do the search?"

row of lockers. "We'll lock it up right there and you can keep the key."

Doc said nothing.

"Perhaps it would be better if you allowed him to do that himself," Ace said.

"Nothing doing."

"Look," Ace said, patting his fingers on his chest. "You guys know me, all the times I've been here. Johnny's not going to be happy if you chase away one of his favorite clients."

"What's in the bag, big man?" the hood asked, pointing toward the valise in Doc's left hand.

Again, Doc said nothing and Ace intervened.

"It's Mr. Markham's gambling money, for Pete's sake." Ace frowned and looked at the hood's face, and then turned to Doc.

"Goliath, would you mind showing them, please?"

Doc stood impassively for several seconds, then stuck the revolver into his belt while he opened the bag to display the money.

One of the hoods emitted a low whistle.

"See what I mean?" Ace said, his handsome face stretching into an ingratiating grin. "Johnny called and specifically asked me to bring Mr. Markham out here to the Lucky Lady. Now, if you don't mind…"

The hood gestured with the pistol toward the lockers and stepped out of Doc's way. He placed the revolver into the slotted opening and retained the key.

"All's well that ends well," Ace said, as he ushered them toward the stairs that led to the gambling rooms. "Is Johnny in his office?"

The hood grunted a reply.

"Good," Ace said. "Call him and tell him we'll see him in a bit."

"After I win some of his money," Deagan called out in his best Texas drawl as he lit up a huge cigar.

When they were out of the hood's earshot, Doc nodded toward a dark corner in the stairwell. They assembled there and he used the hidden zipper to open the false bottom of the case. He handed the pistols to Deagan and Assante and then tucked one in his own beltline.

"This is a massive ship," he said. "If they're holding Miss Cartier and Dr. Jennings onboard, finding them could be a problematic task."

"Which is why we need to do a direct assault," Deagan said. "Just like we did on that castle that time. Go right in and grab the head man. Make him tell us where they got 'em and what's what."

"Crudely put," Ace said, "but quite apt. I agree."

"As do I." Doc nodded toward the staircase and they proceeded down to the main level. The stairway opened up into a massive gaming room with bright floral wallpaper depicting nude mermaids and cartoonish fish, all smiling. Huge nets hung suspended from the juncture between the ceiling and walls, and a huge plaster statue of Neptune surrounded by a massive sea shell decorated the far end. The tables, roulette wheels, and slot machines were all crowded with people as scantily clad cocktail waitresses and cigarette girls moved in and out of the crowds. At least four bars were placed strategically throughout the room, and at the opposite end of the Neptune statue, a woman in an elegant purple evening gown mellifluously sang "Begin the Beguine" into a standing microphone as an orchestra played behind her.

"Ah," Ace said, swaying his head to the music. "That's one of my favorite tunes."

"Figures," Deagan said. "Cole Porter was an odd duck, too."

Ace pointed toward the opposite end of the long room. A stairway adjacent to the orchestra pit led up to a second level. Lights from some kind of room shone through a set of windows shielded by blinds.

As Doc and company approached the stairway they were met by a trio of burly men in dark suits. From the heaviness under their left armpits, it was apparent that each was wearing a shoulder rig with a weapon encased. The largest of the trio held up his hand.

"Can't nobody go up there," he said.

"Apparently you don't know who I am," Deagan said, his voice rife with irritation.

The hood shook his head.

"This is Mr. Markham," Ace chimed in from the other side. "And I'm a personal friend of Johnny's. He's expecting us."

The three hoodlums exchanged glances. "He didn't say nothing to us about it."

Ace raised his eyebrows. "Well, perhaps you'd better check with him."

The hoodlum's mouth twitched and he looked at the other two, who shrugged.

"Wait here," the big hood said, and trotted up the stairs.

Deagan and Ace exchanged glances, and nodded. Both men pivoted quickly, delivering two perfectly timed overhand punches to the jaws of the remaining hoods. They dropped like two ragdolls. Doc removed some special wire restraints and secured the unconscious hoodlums. Deagan removed two pistols from the hoods and held the guns up.

Shrugging, he stuck both of them into his belt. "I can always use a few more."

Doc and Deagan rushed up the stairway, with Ace managing as best he could to ascend as well. They reached the top and another hood sat in a chair outside a closed office door. He looked up as Doc and Deagan approached.

"Where's the toilet?" Deagan asked, a wide grin plastered on his face.

"Huh?" the hood asked.

"Never mind." Deagan swung a clubbing left hook knocking the man to the floor. He bent over the fallen hoodlum, stripped him of his weapon, and then secured his hands behind his back. Just as he was finishing, the big hood from downstairs opened the office door and did a double take.

"What the hell?" he muttered.

Doc dropped the man with an uppercut and stepped over his prone body and into the office.

A portly man in a three-piece gray suit sat behind a large, teakwood desk. His jaw dropped as Doc, Deagan, and Ace entered.

"How yah doin', Johnny?" Ace said.

"Hey." Johnny DeMarco got to his feet. "Youse got no rights coming in here."

"Stow it," Deagan said.

"Is that any way for an Army man to talk?" Ace said with a smile.

Deagan smirked. "I figured I'd use a nautical expression since we're on board."

"Get the hell outta here," DeMarco yelled. "Frankie, Vince, get in here now."

"They're a little busy," Deagan said. "It's just the four of us."

DeMarco's mouth twisted into a scowl.

"You guys are dead meat. You hear me? Dead me—"

Deagan shoved the heavyset gangster back into his chair. It squealed in metallic protest.

DeMarco's face darkened. "I'll kill you for that, buster."

"I don't think so," Deagan replied. He balled up his big fist and started to draw back his right arm, but Doc put a hand on Deagan's shoulder.

Removing his heavy-brimmed hat, Doc stared at DeMarco.

"Tell us immediately the whereabouts of Dr. Walter Jennings and Miss Penelope Cartier. Are they on board this ship?"

"Huh? I got no idea what yer talkin' about." DeMarco tried to move forward to pull open the desk drawer, but Deagan shoved him back and opened the drawer himself. He pulled out a small, silver colored semi-automatic pistol with pearl handle grips.

"My sister used to carry one of these," Deagan said. "'Til she got herself a *real* gun." He slipped the automatic into his pocket.

"How are you involved with this Dark Destroyer business," Doc asked, "and why did you send those men to assassinate me?"

DeMarco's eyes widened, the corners of his mouth turning downward. "Atlas… I shoulda' known." The tip of his tongue moved quickly over his lips, and then he shook his head vehemently. "I got nothing to say to you. Nothing."

Doc stared at the man for a solid ten seconds.

"Calling the cops ain't gonna do you no good, Atlas." DeMarco emitted a harsh laugh. "They ain't got no jurisdiction here, and from what I know about you, you ain't about to shoot me or nothing. You're one of the goody, goody guys." A sly smile curled the lips of his porcine face.

"We are running short of time," Doc said in a calm voice. "I suggest you tell me what you know immediately, lest you run the risk of further charges."

DeMarco uttered a harsh, two-word reply.

Doc showed no emotion to the insult.

"See here, Johnny," Ace said, leaning forward. "You'd best tell us everything. Otherwise, even an attorney as good as me won't be able to keep you out of prison."

DeMarco smirked and repeated the two-word obscenity.

Deagan gripped the front of DeMarco's shirt and literally lifted the fat man out of his chair.

"Just give me five minutes alone with this SOB," Deagan said. "I'll get the answers out of him."

DeMarco's breath came in short gasps.

Doc replaced the hat on his head and motioned for Ace to accompany him out of the room.

Ace shook his head. "Nice knowing you, Johnny."

As they headed for the door DeMarco's voice sounded pinched and nasally. "Hey, where you guys going?"

No response came from Doc or Assante.

"Hey," DeMarco said, his voice rising another octave. "Come back here. Don't leave me alone with this ape."

Deagan pulled DeMarco's face an inch from his own. "What did you call me?"

The two men were eyeball to eyeball for a several more seconds, leaving enough time for Doc to open the office door and start to exit. Then De-Marco cried out: "Okay, okay, wait. I'll talk."

Deagan held the man's gaze, their faces only millimeters apart now. "You'd better start talkin' fast, butterball. Or I'm gonna open you up like a ten cent can of spam."

Doc and Ace stopped at the door.

DeMarco's face flushed as red as a tomato.

"Okay, listen, see…" He licked his lips again. "We're all on the same side here. I'm working in secret with the G, just like Lucky and Big Al did during the War."

• • •

Doc's big sedan shot along the dark roadway bracketed on either side by dense woods. Deagan was at the wheel while Doc sat turned in the passenger seat looking back at the bound figure of Johnny DeMarco. Ace sat next to him with an unlighted cigarette between his fingers.

"Let me know when I can light this up, Doc," Ace said. From his tone it was obvious he needed the tobacco to assuage his nervousness.

Doc didn't reply.

"You know Doc don't want nobody smoking around him," Deagan said over his shoulder.

"Just drive," Ace shot back.

Before Deagan could reply, Doc's voice iced through the darkness. "That's enough. Ace, it would not be prudent to smoke at this time."

"It's a good thing you were a pilot instead of an infantryman," Deagan said. "You and your smokes woulda' been a sniper's dream."

Doc addressed DeMarco: "Describe those government agents again."

"One guy's a big one. Looks sorta like a Kraut, or a Polack. The other one's small, dark, with a face only a rat's mother could love."

"Sounds like our two friends, Agents Smith and Pauls," Ace said. He fingered the cigarette nervously.

"And you're certain they have both Dr. Jennings and Miss Cartier with them?"

DeMarco nodded, his head going up and down like a yo-yo. "That's what they told me. The guys that are buying the death ray demanded that they turn over that Jennings guy, too."

"And Miss Cartier?"

DeMarco's corpulent body shrugged. "I guess they're tossing her in for the ride."

"The ride?" Ace grabbed DeMarco's ear and twisted. "Where were you supposed to take her?"

DeMarco grunted in pain. "Leggo, leggo. I told yah, after I meet them out here, we're going back to the Lucky Lady and I'm to head down to Havana. There's another ship waiting down there."

Doc and Ace exchanged glances. Ace gave the gangster's ear a final twist. "You'd better hope she's all right, you fat pig."

DeMarco said nothing, his breath coming in short gasps.

"We're almost to the airfield, Doc," Deagan said.

"Pull over there, Thomas," Doc said. "Behind those trees where the vehicle won't be seen from the road. And extinguish the headlights. We'll proceed from here on foot."

"What'll we do with him?" Ace asked.

Deagan turned back, his mouth cocked in a crooked grin as the vehicle slowed to a stop. "I'll open the trunk."

After depositing DeMarco, the three of them crept down the highway until they came to a gravel access road.

"Stay along the tree line," Doc said, his voice low.

"More infantry tactics, fly boy," Deagan said. "In case you didn't know."

Ace didn't reply.

Perhaps fifty yards ahead the silhouette of a long sedan was visible. Two men, one large, the other smaller, stood smoking by the front fender.

"See what I mean?" Deagan said, slapping Assante on the arm. "They're perfect targets."

Ace didn't answer.

Doc drew his pistol, as did Ace and Deagan, who had a gun in each hand. Through the collected shrubbery Doc could see the two men by the vehicle with more clarity. They were definitely the two men who had appeared at his office that morning, Dexter Smith and Arthur Pauls. The silhouettes of two other people in the car were also visible, one of them appeared to be a woman. They crept closer and Doc signaled them to squat down as the buzz from an approaching engine became audible. Twin headlights illuminated the roadway as a truck wound its way along the gravel road coming toward them.

The truck rumbled past, pulled up to the sedan, and stopped. The doors opened and three men got out. Two more men jumped down from the rear bed of the truck. These two carried rifles.

"Looks like we're a little out gunned," Ace whispered.

"Lemme at 'em," Deagan growled. "I think one of them's the one that sapped me in D.C."

"Our primary goal is to ensure the safety of the hostages," Doc said. "Ace, that'll be your job. Thomas and I will engage the others."

Assante nodded.

The men had gathered in front of the vehicles now, talking in animated conversation. The smaller man, Pauls, quickly walked to the rear of the truck, accompanied by one of the riflemen. Pauls shone a flashlight inside.

"Looking good, Dex," he called out.

"Let's do it," Deagan said.

He and Doc immediately sprang up and began a quick advance. Doc covered the distance with incredible speed, coming up on the rifleman and the ferret-like Pauls before they could even turn. Doc clipped the man holding the rifle squarely across the bridge of the nose with the side of his pistol. With his left hand, Doc shot out a short, but powerful, punch that collided with Pauls' jaw. The little man's head bounced off the metal tailgate of the truck and he crumpled. Deagan brought the barrel of one of his forty-fives down on the head of the stunned rifleman. This man fell also. Replacing the pistols in his belt, Deagan grabbed the man's long gun and immediately checked the breech. Slamming the bolt back into place, he nodded and headed around the right side of the truck.

Doc flattened against the big vehicle's left side and edged toward the group of men at the front. He canted his head slightly to check on Ace's progress. Assante had made it to the rear of the sedan. One man stood by the front fender, a gun dangling loosely in his hand.

Ace brought his pistol up and the man turned suddenly, also bringing his gun to bear.

The flame from Ace's pistol tore through the dark night, accompanied by the roaring explosion of the round going off. The man at the front of the sedan jerked backward and disappeared. Smith and the other men in front of the truck turned and raised their guns.

Doc drew a bead on the man with the rifle and squeezed off two rounds, one to the head and one to the chest. The man fell forward. The other two men ran and Smith extended his gun toward Doc. The blast from Deagan's rifle tore through the night and Smith's head momentarily jerked to the side. Doc squeezed off another round, catching Smith in the body. The big man grunted and stumbled forward, the gun dropping from his fingers. The other men ran in a zigzagging pattern away from the vehicles, firing their weapons as they moved. Rounds shattered the windows in the truck and plunked against the metallic surface. The reports from Deagan's rifle, the rounds evenly spaced, offered a punctuation of sorts, and then all the firing ceased.

Deagan went to check on the fallen men. Doc stepped forward and kicked the gun away from Smith's outstretched hand. The man grunted in pain.

"Atlas," he said. "Help me. I'm shot."

Doc said nothing. Instead, he looked back toward the sedan where he saw Ace holding Penny in an embrace. Assante smiled and gave a thumbs-up.

Doc checked on Deagan's progress, then knelt to check on Smith's wound. The bullet had entered the man's side and appeared to be a through-and-through, although there would be a danger of a collapsing lung.

"It looks survivable," Doc said. "You should pull through."

"You're supposed to be a doctor," Smith said, his words laced with pain. "Do something."

"I am," Doc said, taking out a knife and cutting away the man's jacket and shirt. "We'll get you to a hospital shortly. Now, fill in the blanks for me. Who were these men, and what's in that truck."

Smith's breath came out in ragged gasps. "They're Russians, you idiot. The truck's full of gold bullion."

Doc shone his flashlight over the wound. The blood flow was constant, but not pulsating. "Gold? For what purpose?"

Smith swallowed hard, shook his head.

"Talk, if you want me to help you," Doc said.

"All right, all right," Smith said. "They're Soviet agents. They were supposed to be buying the plans for Tesla's death ray."

"Which does not exist."

Smith grimaced. "Yeah, it was all faked."

Deagan was at their side now, shining his flashlight on the wound site so Doc could use both hands. He ripped the man's shirt into strips and began using them as a make-shift bandage.

"A fake?" Deagan said. "But what about that boat he blew up?"

Smith said nothing.

Doc answered for him: "The boat was rigged with an explosive charge, most likely set off by a radio transmission. They most likely used a powerful light beam to simulate the death ray." He paused and Smith nodded reluctantly. Doc continued: "The two bodies that were recovered from the water had dentition that showed prolonged and extreme neglect. Most likely they were abducted from the Bowery and killed prior to the explosion."

This time Smith said nothing.

"And that Dark Destroyer guy?" Deagan asked.

"There was no Dark Destroyer," Doc said, "Only a false G-man with a flair for the theatrical. And an unfortunate streak of avarice."

"You're wrong, Atlas," Smith said. "We ain't crooks. We're patriots. We had this whole death ray thing set up as a diversion to keep the Soviets busy working on a whole lot of nothing instead of trying to develop their own A-bomb."

Ace walked over with Jennings and Penny. She held the front of her dress closed and glared down at the wounded charlatan.

"Jennings spilled it all to me while we were being driven up here," Penny said. "They were going to deliver Tesla's worthless papers to the Reds. And they were going to toss us in as a bargain." She drew her leg back and kicked Smith's side. He grunted in pain.

"Don't do that, Miss Cartier," Doc said. "This man is no longer an imminent threat."

"Oh, I think he is," she shot back. "Him and his buddy are ex-OSS. Once Truman disbanded their little organization, they saw a chance to make themselves rich."

"No," Smith said. "We're patriots. Doing what has to be done in today's world. You may not like it, but that gold was going to fund a new intelligence branch of the government."

"I hate to be the bearer of bad news, pal," Ace said. "One of the bullets tore through the canvas covering on the truck. That *gold bullion* is pure lead, covered by thin, gold plating. Looks like both you and the Reds were chasing your tails."

Deagan laughed. "For once, fly-boy, I'm happy to hear you get the last word."

Doc finished tying off the make-shift bandages and stood, lifting Smith as effortlessly as if he were picking up a suitcase.

"Gather up those bodies and place them in the truck," he said. "We've got to notify the proper authorities."

"And I've gotta get to a phone," Penny said. "This has page-one written all over it."

Doc allowed the trace of smile to grace his lips. He knew that the real story would no doubt be suppressed by the government, but the girl had been through a lot.

And she was rather attractive. He wondered if he'd see her again.

Perhaps I shall, he thought, *as long as she and Ace were no longer dating…*

The End

But…
Doc Atlas will return…

WHO IS DOC ATLAS?

Doc Atlas is one of the few mystery men who needs no secret identity; one who operates with the blessings of local law and federal authorities; who fought valiantly with his companions Mad Dog Deagan and Ace Assante in WW II. Co-creators and co-authors Michael A. Black and Ray Lovato wanted to explore Doc's transition back into civilian life and look at how he established his base of operations to begin his crusade against a new brand of villainy. Several years ago, Black and Lovato met for a Doc Atlas Summit outside of Palm Springs, California, dedicating three days to exploring the world of possibilities for the Golden Avenger. Incredible plots, concepts and outlines for Doc and his crew, all placed within actual historical time frames, were hatched.

Born out of this brain storming session was the idea of having Doc interact with the life's work of Nicola Tesla, genius inventor of the early 20th century. Tesla's legacy includes his claim of perfecting a "Death Ray" capable of destroying enemy aircraft many miles away. Upon Tesla's death, the F.B.I. confiscated all of his life's research. The papers were examined for weeks at M.I.T. and then sent to the Department of the Navy for storage. Michael and Ray knew that there was a Doc Atlas adventure waiting in these historical facts. The co-authors have been life-long friends since that fateful day they met when they were six years old. And these many years later, both of them say that plotting and writing the incredible adventures of Doc Atlas has kept them forever young.

Ray would like to dedicate this work to the angel who watches over him every day, his lovely wife Susan. And to his best friend who has saved his life on many occasions, Mike Black.

Visit our websites: doc-atlas.com MichaelABlack.com and The Incredible Adventures of Doc Atlas: The Doc Atlas Omnibus on FACEBOOK. Read Doc's other adventures, *Melody of Vengeance* and *The Incredible Adventures of Doc Atlas*, available on Amazon.com.

• • •

MICHAEL A. BLACK - is the author of twenty books and over one-hundred short stories and articles. His latest novel is *Chimes at Midnight* and he is also writing the Mack Bolan Executioner series (*Sleeping Dragons, Deadly Salvage, Payback*).

RAYMOND LOUIS JAMES LOVATO loves writing pulp fiction with his lifelong friend author Michael A. Black. Ray also enjoys traveling the world with his lovely wife, Susan. Years ago, on a five-hour flight to Saint Martin, he was inspired to draft an homage to Doc Savage, the Man of Bronze. After presenting the first chapter as a serial birthday gift to his best friend, the Adventures of Doc Atlas was born. Black wrote the first Doc Atlas novel, A MELODY OF VENGEANCE, as a tribute to the Pulp Age of Heroes.